DELIGHTS TO CHERISH

DELIGHTS TO CHERISH

Dhinakaran

2019

Delights To Cherish – published by the Rev. Dr. Ashish Amos of the Indian Society for Promoting Christian Knowledge (ISPCK), Post Box 1585, Kashmere Gate, Delhi-110006.

Online order: http://ispck.org.in/book.php

Also available on amazon.in

ISBN: 978-93-88945-05-9

Laser typeset by

ISPCK, Post Box 1585, 1654, Madarsa Road, Kashmere Gate, Delhi-110006 • *Tel:* 23866323

e-mail: ashish@ispck.org.in • ella@ispck.org.in
website: www.ispck.org.in

Dedicated to

K.S. Savariyar - Jesintha Selva Rani

Sr. Jayabharathi

Josephine Sahaya Mary – Darwin

Amalanathan

Sijo, Infanta, Jijo

Contents

Contents

Contents

Preface

Story is a common art form. If the world is made up of atoms scientifically, it is made up of stories existentially. All scriptures, traditions, cultures, moral instructions and teachings take recourse to stories to entertain, educate, inspire and instruct. Life is more effectively explained through stories. Although they are renditions of the past, their echoes transcend the timeline and prove ever relevant to human life. It is thus that they aid our pursuit of wisdom in life. With their didactic and inspirational elements, stories become the treasure trove for the wisdom seekers in terms of motivation and enlightenment.

The book is a collection of a hundred anecdotes from both history and tradition. I had tried to adapt, abridge and reproduce them from the numerous sources I had relied on to collect. So varied and multiple as they are, they have been culled out from books, newspapers, Google search engine, magazines and films in order to enrich the collection. In this process, I do regret my limitation to substantiate them with proper reference to their sources. However, my intention is to inculcate some of the virtues and values that the stories stand to mean. Points for pro-action at the end of each anecdote have been rendered to illuminate and orient us into deriving lessons from what we cherish. I do wish to find you conversing with them with a relentless hunt to pick something for life. I wish you the best!

1

We Started It Together!
We Will Finish It Together!

At the 1992 Barcelona Olympics, British sprinter Derek Redmond and his father provided audiences with one of the most heart-wrenching moments in Olympic history. Redmond had qualified for the semi-final of the 400m with the fastest time in his heat. He was looking strong when suddenly he pulled up- his hamstring had torn. Rather than crumble to the ground, Redmond continued hobbling towards the finishing line. When all the doctors and officials were trying to get him to stop, he was having none of it.

It is at this time, his dad Jim provided one of the modern-day Olympics' most celebrated and long-lasting images as he burst through security and on to the track to intercept his stricken son, who was dragging himself onwards in floods of tears. At the time of excruciating pain, Derek remembers, 'I became aware of someone else on the track. I didn't realize it was my dad, Jim, at first. He said, 'Derek, it's me, you don't need to do this.' I just said, 'Dad, I want to finish, get me back in the semi-final.' He said, 'Ok. We started this thing together and now we'll finish it together.' He managed to get me to stop trying to run and just walk and he kept repeating, 'You're a champion, you've got nothing to prove.'

Jim and Derek completed the lap of the track together, with Derek leaning on his father's shoulder for support. As they crossed the finishing line, the crowd of 65,000 spectators rose to give Derek a standing ovation. However, as his father had helped him finish, Derek was officially disqualified and Olympic records state that he 'Did Not Finish' the race. However, Derek Redmond will forever be remembered as the athlete who broke down in Barcelona and was helped to the finish line by his father. Later, Redmond's struggle in the 1992 semi-final became the subject of one of the International Olympic Committee's 'Celebrate Humanity' videos, which proclaimed: 'Force is measured in kilograms. Speed is measured in seconds. Courage? You can't measure courage.'

Points for Pro-Action

A friend in a father is a blessing indeed!

Can we deny the existence of roots because they are not as visible as branches and leaves? A father's love in many cases is such; it is a love not so visible; yet so deep as roots!

A father's love is often camouflaged in rigidity! To any outward appearance he is like a pricking thorn on jackfruit.

Let's not get carried away by the externals! A father's inward sweetness is nothing short of the sweetness of the fruit itself.

2

The Courage To Forgive!

On September 11, 2001, Phyllis Rodriguez's son, Greg, was killed in the terrorist attacks on the World Trade Center. Two months later, Aicha el-Wafi's son, Zacarias Moussaou, was indicted on charges of conspiring to plan the attack. In 2002, the two mothers met. Over the years they have built an unlikely friendship based on forgiveness, peace, and hope for the future. Rodriguez said: 'When Greg was killed, I thought I will never forgive the people who murdered my son, but I have come to see forgiveness as more than a word; it's a context, a process. I don't forgive the act but trying to understand why someone has acted in the way they have is part of the process of forgiving. Forgiveness is being able to accept another person for being human and fallible.' She further added 'When I watched Zacarias at the trial my heart was broken because I could not look at him as a stranger. I saw him as the son of my friend Aicha. However, when people heard that my son was a victim, I got immediate sympathy. But when people learned what her son was accused of, she didn't get that sympathy. But her suffering is equal to mine. She is a mother like me. I suffered a lot as a mother. For all the women, all the mothers that give life, you can give it back. You can change. It's up to us women, because we are women because we love our children.' On her part, Aicha is silently enduring the pain of conviction of her son while at the same she never condones his behaviour; rather she desires to have peace in the world with no hatred and violence. Both said: 'We have tried to know other people, the other you have to be generous and your hearts must be generous. Your mind must be generous. You must be tolerant. You must fight against violence. And I hope that someday we will all live together in peace and respect each other.'

Their example is truly inspiring in what it can mean and in what it can bring about. Both could go beyond their pain and accept each other without judging whose fault it was all about. They are far from the majority that rushes to judge the other and garners pleasure out of branding the other. When there is real love and mercy, we meet the other in their vulnerability and start loving them for what they are. They both have proved that in our strength we are admired; but in our vulnerability we are loved. All it takes is a merciful heart to truly love the other and prove human.

Points for Pro-Action

Forgiveness is linked to a refusal to condemn. It is a non-judgemental attitude towards oneself and others. We dare not condemn others because there is evil in all of us.

We are not to judge because we cannot read human hearts. But let us not forget that forgiveness cannot bypass justice. It demands it. True forgiveness includes the desire and the will to re-establish justice when harm has been done.

Forgiveness is not the approval or a condoning of evil, whether personal or social. It does not excuse or tolerate evil; rather, it overcomes that. It does not advocate passivity in the face of injustice but invites us not to retaliate for evil, but to surpass it through constructive action.

Because of all these, forgiveness is not an act of the weak; it is rather the act of the strong.

3

Virtue of The Heart!

When Thane Cyclone having 140 kmph of wind speed hit Tamilnadu and Puducherry in December 2011, it left a trail of death and destruction. At least 33 people were killed and the devastation to properties and agriculture was unprecedented. Century-old trees were uprooted, and houses and buildings met with destruction hitherto unknown. The impact was so fiercely felt that the level of devastation forced the cyclone-hit areas into nearly a decade of backwardness. However, such a natural calamity was not without its blessings in terms of humanitarian outreach and solidarity with those affected by the cyclone.

Notable among them was the example of Asina Parvin who became well-known for her generosity even though she was just a primary school girl. The seven-year-old donated Rs. 3,052 that she had saved in her piggy bank to buy a cycle to victims of Thane cyclone. When she heard of the cyclone disaster that disrupted many families, she told her father she wanted to give away her savings to help the victims. She could buy a cycle later, she reasoned. On learning about her generosity, TI cycles came forward to present Asina her dream cycle. Asina's father Sheik Dawood, an electrician, and her homemaker mother Pathimuthu were very happy about their little angel.

Points for Pro-Action

Real giving is ***not giving from*** what we have; but ***all that we have***.

It is the joy of the giver that benefits the receiver; a grumbling giver spoils the gift.

Charity is a virtue of the heart, not of the hand.

What matters in charity is the size of the heart; ultimately, a generous heart is nobler than swollen heads.

4

Two Hardest Tests on Spiritual Road!

Nasiruddin arranged to give a lecture at two o'clock in the afternoon, and it looked set to be a great success: the thousand seats were completely sold out and more than seven hundred people were left outside.

At two o'clock precisely, an assistant of Nasiruddin's came in, saying that, for unavoidable reasons, the lecture would begin late. Some got up indignantly, asked for their money back and left. Even so, a lot of people remained both inside and outside the lecture hall.

By four in the afternoon, the Sufi master had still not appeared, and people gradually began to leave the place, picking up their money at the box office. The working day was coming to an end, it was time to go home. When it was six o'clock the original one thousand seven hundred spectators had dwindled to less than a hundred.

At that moment, Nasiruddin came in. He appeared to be extremely drunk and unsteady that he fell with a thud on the floor. Astonished, the people who had remained behind began to feel indignant. How could the man behave like that after making them wait for four hours? There were some disapproving murmurs, but the Sufi master ignored them. After cursing the people who were complaining, Nasiruddin tried to get up, but again fell heavily to the floor. Disgusted, more people decided to leave.

Now only nine people remained. As soon as the final group of outraged spectators had left, Nasiruddin got up; he was completely sober, his eyes glowed, and he had about him an air of great authority and wisdom.

'Those of you who stayed are the ones who will hear me' he said. 'You have passed through the two hardest tests on the spiritual road; the patience to wait for the right moment and the courage not to be disappointed with what you encounter. It is you I will teach.'

Points for Pro-Action

Patience is not passive waiting; but it is waiting with hope.

Patience also means to rely on God's providence more than placing inordinate and unrealistic trust in one's ability.

Courage is not without fear; but it is fear that prays.

True courage is the virtue of one who refuses to abandon in the face of threat.

5

Peace Pilgrim!

There is an inspiring story about Mildred Lisette Norman who wanted to be known as Peace Pilgrim. She chose to walk across the United States for 28 years covering more than 40,000 km (25,000 miles) for peace. Her pilgrimage spanned almost three decades beginning on January 1, 1953, in Pasadena, California. Her long march through the length and breadth of the country served as a reminder against the country's involvement in Korean as well as Vietnam Wars.

During her journey, Peace Pilgrim was a frequent speaker at churches, universities, and local and national radio and television. In the book, 'Peace Pilgrim: Her Life and Work in Her Own Words', she related that her physical journey began after having experienced a 'spiritual awakening', following a long period of meditation practice. She said that this awakening was a direct, mystical experience of the 'creator's love.' She claimed that this spurred her to start her decades-long walking journey for peace. Peace Pilgrim's only possessions were the clothes on her back and the few items she carried in the pockets of her blue tunic which read 'Peace Pilgrim' on the front and '25,000 Miles on foot for peace' on the back. She had no organizational backing, carried no money, and would not even ask for food or shelter. When she began her pilgrimage, she had taken a vow to 'remain a wanderer until humankind has learned the way of peace, walking until given shelter and fasting until given food.'

Points for Pro-Action

A task without a vision is drudgery; a vision without a task is reverie; a task with a vision is victory.

If we do only what is required of us, we are slaves; the moment we do more, we are free people.

Age or energy: What are we dictated by?

Every one of us has the power to make someone happy; let's do it. The world needs more of that.

6

One Man Army!

Traffic Ramasamy is a name that is quite familiar to all citizens of Tamil Nadu in general and to all residents of Chennai in particular. A well-known social activist at the age of 77, he is the largest filer of Public Interest Litigations (PILs) in the Madras High Court and he has battled everything from restoring two-way traffic on Chennai roads to reducing illegal buildings and encroachments to rubble. As his family is not so happy with his activism, he has had to live away from his family and of that he has no regrets. On being made fun of for his work and attire and on being discouraged and frowned upon that he would never change the world, he says he does not mind the barbs. 'I have a conscience. I will follow it. I walk with the wads of paper in my two pockets, so that people can recognize me, wherever I go.' He has been beaten up on several occasions for 'disturbing' the public and their comfort. He exhausts his own retirement fund for such philanthropic activities and is sometimes supported by friends and well-wishers. He opines, 'I am one of the lowest middle-class persons. I have no money with me but I'm living.' His life and struggle have been well portrayed in a biographical work entitled, 'One Man Army.'

Points for Pro-Action

The person who struggles is better than the person who never attempts.

Is our social activity merely an act of tokenism?

Are we ever willing to suffer for the love of the other?

The meaning of altruistic love is the denial of oneself in love of the other.

7

Unheard Melodies!

G hulam Dastagir is the unsung hero of Bhopal Gas Tragedy that shook not only India but the entire world by becoming the world's worst industrial disaster releasing 30 tons of highly toxic gas called methyl isocyanate into Bhopal neighbourhood when the entire city was asleep. While exposing 600,000 people to the poisonous gas, the tragedy left countless dead and many others breathless, blind and agonizing in pain. On that fateful night – 2 December 1984, when the city of Bhopal was hit by the industrial catastrophe, the deputy station master of Bhopal railway station Ghulam Dastagir risked his own life to save countless lives. The list of dead people is a little shorter thanks to his gesture of goodwill that ensured the safety of many.

On finding his stationmaster Harish Dhurve dead along with 23 of his companions and himself experiencing the burning of eyes and a queer itching sensation, he felt he had no time to spare and sprang into action to save others. Helped by a swift sense of judgement, he ordered the early departure of Gorakhpur Mumbai Express although it was 20 minutes earlier. Besides that, he alerted the senior staff at nearby stations, like Vidisha and Itarsi, to suspend all train traffic to Bhopal. Unfortunately, that was not all; situations kept getting worse with the passage of time. The railway station was fast filling up with people desperate to flee the fumes. Some were gasping, others were vomiting, and most were weeping. But risking his life, Dastagir chose to remain on duty, running from one platform to another, attending, helping and consoling victims while arranging for medical help.

Dastagir stayed at the station, steadfastly doing his duty, fully aware that his family was out there in the ill-fated city. Although his sense of duty and commitment saved countless lives, one of his sons died on the night of the tragedy and another developed a lifelong skin infection. Dastagir himself spent his last 19 years shuttling in and out of hospitals; he developed a painful growth in the throat due to prolonged exposure to toxic fumes. Indian railways have put up a memorial on the platform of the Bhopal station but Ghulam Dastagir's name is not on the list. He is the forgotten hero who went out of his way to save the lives of unknown people at the cost of his own health and family's well being.

Points for Pro-Action

A hero is an ordinary individual who finds strength to persevere and endure despite overwhelming obstacles.

World can never afford to forget its heroes by whose sacrifices we sustain ourselves.

We make a living by what we get; but we make a life by what we give – Winston Churchill.

I have found that among its other benefits, giving liberates the soul of the giver – Maya Angelou.

8

The Story Behind 'The Burning Desire!'

The Brooklyn Bridge that spans the river connecting Manhattan Island to Brooklyn is truly a miracle bridge. In 1863, a creative engineer named John Roebling was inspired by an idea for this spectacular bridge. However, bridge-building experts throughout the world told him to forget it; it could not be done.

Roebling convinced his son Washington, the young up-coming engineer that the bridge could be built. Two of them developed the concepts of how it could be accomplished and how the obstacles could be overcome. With harnessed excitement and inspiration, they hired their crew and began to build their dream bridge.

The project was only a few months under construction when a tragic accident on the site took the life of John Roebling and severely injured his son, Washington who was further left with permanent brain damage and was unable to talk or walk. Everyone felt that the project would have to be scrapped since the Roebling's were the only ones who knew how the bridge could be built.

Even though Washington was unable to move or talk, his mind was as sharp as ever and his heart harbored the burning desire to complete the bridge. An idea hit him as he lay in his hospital bed, and he developed a code for communication.

All he could move was one finger, so he touched the arm of his wife with that little finger, tapping out the code to communicate to her what to tell the engineers who were building the bridge. For thirteen years, Washington tapped out his instructions with his finger until the spectacular Brooklyn Bridge was finally completed.

Points for Pro-Action

Real disability is not often physical. It is what we keep telling ourselves that impairs us.

Failure is not the final word when there is hope alive even amidst discouragement and disapproval.

Ability is what we can do. Motivation determines what we do. Attitude determines how well we do it.

The happiness of our life depends on the quality of our thoughts.

9

The Fragrance of Reconciliation!

No Indian would have ever forgotten the two faces of Gujarat Communal riots 2002: A Muslim by name Ansari who was seen with tears begging for life and Ashok Mochi with a saffron band around his head, a rod in one hand and the other clinched into a fist. One could remember through these iconic personalities the Gujarat communal riots in which according to realistic estimates other than official records of the government, as many as more than 2000 Muslims were killed, more than 300 went missing, and 2500 injured. India witnessed one of the worst scenes of intolerance and enmity. However, my intention is not to make you relive the horror.

My purpose here is to take you all to focus on Mar 4, 2014, a red-letter day in the Indian history not because something of national importance transpired but because a real act forgiveness and reconciliation took place between Mochi and Ansari, the two iconic personalities who reminded the world of the Gujarat carnage back in 2002. They both were invited by Kerala Marxist Communist Party to exchange peace and brotherhood so that the wounds behealed. When the victimizer and the victim of Gujarat Communal violence met and hugged each other as friends, one could witness a beautiful moment of history, a moment of forgiveness, of healing between the two.

Points for Pro-Action

In failures and betrayal, we reveal human weakness; but in forgiveness we reveal the glimpse of the divine in us.

One should have courage to disown the disabling past and say 'yes' to the empowering future.

If we don't open ourselves to what is liberating, we become doomed to slavery.

In forgiveness it is not that we heal others; rather we heal ourselves.

10

A Heart With No Compunction

In November 2007, one of the American dailies came out with this news: 'Pilot who dropped atomic bomb on Hiroshima dies with no regrets.' The entire world was startled at the unperturbed manner with which he faced his death. Moreover, to his dying day, the experienced pilot insisted he never lost a single's night sleep over the apocalyptic mission and that his main concern was to do the 'best job' he could.

Paul Tibbets who had flown some of the first bombing missions over Germany during World War II, dropped the bomb on Hiroshima from B-29 bomber Enola Gay on August 6. Nicknamed 'Little Boy' the bomb killed 78,000 people instantly but by the end of 1945 the death total had reached 140,000. After the mission Mr. Tibbets said: 'If Dante had been with us on the plane, he would have been terrified. The city we had seen so clearly in the sunlight a few minutes before was now an ugly smudge. It had completely disappeared under this awful blanket of smoke and fire.'

He stated in an interview with newspaper the Columbus Dispatch in 1975: 'I'm not proud that I killed 80,000 people, but I'm proud that I was able to start with nothing, plan it and have it work as perfectly as it did.' He went on to justify, 'You've got to take stock and assess the situation at that time. We were at war. You use anything at your disposal. We had feelings, but we had to put them in the background. My one concern was to do the best job I could, so we could end the killing as quickly as possible. He added, it was his patriotic duty – 'to do the right thing.'

In talking about Tibbets, our attempt is not to hold only Tibbets culpable but all who were responsible for planning the heart-breaking massacre of reducing humans to mere play things to be tested upon. However, what disappoints us is his conscience that felt no qualm about what he had done although he could 'take pride' in a 'job' well done!

Points for Pro-Action

We have the gift of conscience to guide us in matters of consequence. Are we able to differentiate the voice of God within?

Asking a pardon is the art of lightening the heart that is writhing with the burden of guilt.

In trying to save embarrassment, we harden our hearts that in course of time it can become insensitive even to the blunders we might commit one day.

Acknowledging one's guilt is simultaneous conversion.

11

The Modern Good Samaritan!

Auto Raja is an unforgettable name for the citizens of Bengaluru. Turning from a rogue to a saint, his transformation has been helpful not only to him as an individual, but to the society as well.

His prison experience gave him the impetus to realize the miseries of human life whereupon he vowed to alleviate human misery even in little ways possible for him. Later, when he became an auto driver, his rides across the Bengaluru city exposed him to the sight of the inhabitants of obscure street corners – unkempt beggars, mentally ill people who have been thrown out of homes, destitute women, children and elders. Their appalling living conditions drove him to come out with something constructive as against the little charity that he could afford from his meagre income – from providing food and water to bed sheets and clothes. It was when he decided to initiate some relief measure on a larger scale that opening of 'Home of Hope' came to his mind and it is a reality today.

His service that stretches into two decades and more has done immense good to the society that he stands tall as a figure of inspiration to many who would like to contribute to the society constructively. The lone mission he began two decades back has found enormous support from all sections of the society that the government, NGOs, donors and well-wishers joined hands with him to make his mission noble and meaningful.

He has rescued over 10,000 beggars and destitute from the streets of Bengaluru in the past 20 years. The Home of Hope that he began with just 13 inmates has grown into an asylum for nearly 750 people – all picked from the streets. 80 percent of the people rescued by him are mentally challenged and he has cremated nearly 4000 dead bodies lying on the streets in the past 20 years.

Quoting Mother Teresa as model and example for his mission, he desires to match her in commitment and love towards tending to the 'invalids' of the society. A person of various accolades, awards and recognitions, Auto Raja humbly admits that 'What I do is God's work and I am just an instrument in His mission.'

Points for Pro-Action

Every one of us is responsible for all the rest of us who have been denied love and care as humans.

The throwaway culture that began with things has sadly ended with humans that it is high time we gave expression to the humanity frozen in each one of us.

Let's become more neighbourly that no 'throw away' person of the society escapes our 'searching' eyes.

Let us get rid of the stigma of oppression and begin an era of real brotherhood/sisterhood.

12

World, Take My Son by The Hand!

One of the world's most beautiful letters written in the history is that which Abraham Lincoln wrote to his son's teacher requesting him to inculcate in his son the values that would keep his head high amidst life's hard realities and vicissitudes. The ideas of the letter are universally appealing to all the parents reflecting their hearts' desire to have their children educated in ways recommended by Lincoln and it is because of its universal appeal that the world goes back upon to cherish its value and greatness. One of the versions of his letter goes like this:

'World take my child by the hand-he starts school today!

It is all going to be strange and new to him for a while, and I wish you would sort of treat him gently. You see, up to now, he has been king of the roost. He has been the boss of the backyard. I have always been around to repair his wounds, and I have always been handy to soothe his feelings.

But now things are going to be different. This morning he is going to walk down the front steps, wave his hand, and start on a great adventure that probably will include wars and tragedy and sorrow.

To live in this world will require faith and love and courage. So, World, I wish you would sort of take him by his young hand and teach him the things he will have to know. Teach him-but gently, if you can.

He will have to learn, I know, that all people are not just and that all men and women are not true. Teach him that for every scoundrel, there is a hero; that for every enemy, there is a friend. Let him learn early that the bullies are the easiest people to lick.

Teach him the wonder of books. Give him quiet time to ponder the eternal mystery of birds in the sky, bees in the sun, and flowers on a green hill. Teach him that it is far more honourable to fail than to cheat. Teach him to have faith in his own ideas, even if everyone tells him they are wrong.

Try to give my son the strength not to follow the crowd when everyone else is getting on the bandwagon. Teach him to listen to others, but to filter all he hears on a screen of truth and to take only the good that comes through.

Teach him never to put a price tag on his heart and soul. Teach him to close his ears on the howling mob-and to stand and fight if he thinks he is right. Teach him gently, World, but do not coddle him, because only the test of fire makes fine steel.

This is a big order, World, but see what you can do. He is such a nice son.'

Points for Pro-Action

Teachers affect eternity; no one can tell where their influence stops – Henry Brooks Adams.

A good teacher is a gift to the humanity, a credit to the society and a blessing to the pupils.

Teachers sculpt the students more by their life than by their knowledge.

Teaching is the one profession that creates all other professions.

13

One Thing Can Change Everything!

During World War II (1939-1945), the Battle of Normandy (which lasted from June 1944 to August 1944) secured a unique attention because it resulted in the Allied liberation of Western Europe from Nazi Germany's control. Codenamed Operation Overlord, the battle began on June 6, 1944, when some 156,000 American, British and Canadian forces landed on five beaches along a 50-mile stretch of the heavily fortified coast of France's Normandy region. Also known as D-Day, the invasion was one of the largest amphibious military assaults in history and required extensive planning.

It is no exaggeration if we claim that the momentum gained on the D-Day by allied forces changed the course of the Second World War and it was the day the marked the decline and fall of the Nazis. Yet the brave sacrifice of the soldiers remains unmatchable because all of them knew that they were to land on the heavily fortified Normandy coast and as expected more than 10000 lost their lives and thousands of others fatally wounded.

Before D-Day, the Germans were in an enviable position of only having to fight a war on one front: the eastern front, where the Russians were steadily encroaching on the territory Germany had won. Almost since the beginning of the war, Germany was in control of Western Europe, so they had little fear of anything happening militarily from that direction.

Hence, prior to D-Day, the Allies conducted a large-scale deception campaign designed to mislead the Germans about the intended invasion target. Thus, D-Day became the red-letter day in human history. By late August 1944, northern France had been liberated, and by the following spring the Allies had defeated the Germans. The Normandy landings have been called the beginning of the end of war in Europe.

In what it achieved the D-Day became the turning point by simultaneously empowering the allied forces and weakening the strength of the Nazis. As a result, the allied forces started making steady progress against the German forces for more than a year. Hence, what is fair to say is that the tides turned against the German forces at Normandy, shortening the war and giving the Allies momentum on the continent of Europe. The evil of Nazism encountered its defeat by means of the supreme sacrifice of the soldiers who were aware of what was to befall them. In short, D-Day owes everything to the sacrifice of the soldiers.

Points for Pro-Action

It is said of soldiers: Soldiers give their todays for our tomorrows.

There is no greater sacrifice than laying down one's life for others.

The soldiers face death not with grumbling but with willingness. Death can never take them by surprise; they know it comes and move forward to face it.

Life is not taken away from soldiers; rather they choose to give it.

14

Dying for A Cause...!

During his lifetime, when Nelson Mandela was fighting the racist apartheid government and its oppression, he faced arrest on charges of being an outlaw. However, Mandela was ready to die because he knew well that challenging the white racist government and its cherished belief of apartheid would be challenging death itself. 'To be truly prepared for something,' he was to say, 'one must expect it... (Making a mention of his companions and himself, he said) We were all prepared, not because we were brave but because we were realistic.' As he climbed into the armoured police van that would take him to the apartheid court, he thought of these lines from Shakespeare: 'Be absolute for death; either death or life shall thereby be the sweeter.'

Points for Pro-Action

What good is a person's life if he/she can't even choose what to die for – Tony Morrison.

Commitment is a value that calls for absolute readiness and sacrifice.

Sacrifice is done not in fear of threats but in love of convictions.

The brave die once; but the cowards die a thousand times before they really die.

15

Providence of God!

Years ago, in Scotland, the Clark family had a dream to travel to the United States. After years of hard work, they saved money, received passports, and reserved places for the whole family on a new liner to the United States. The family was excited about the trip and meanwhile something happened to dampen their excitement.

Just a week before the departure, the youngest son was bitten by a dog. After treating him, the doctor hung a yellow sheet on Clark's front door because the possibility of rabies was suspected and therefore the entire family was quarantined for fourteen days. Dreams of their dream travel shattered, the father could only helplessly watch the mighty Titanic leaving the dock with tears of disappointment and began to curse God and his son for the misfortune.

Five days later, the tragic news spread throughout Scotland that the 'Unsinkable' and 'Mighty' Titanic had sunk taking hundreds of lives with it. Had the Clark family been on board the ship as planned, they would have perished as well. When Mr. Clark heard the news, he hugged his son and thanked him for saving the family. He thanked God for saving their lives and turning what he had felt was a tragedy into a blessing.

Points for Pro-Action

Not all storms come to disturb our life; some come to clear our path.

A bend in life is not the end in life.

Learn to smile; not because everything is good, but because we can see the good in everything.

Obstacles may be blessings in disguise sometimes.

16

Processionary Caterpillars!

The famous French naturalist, Jean Henry Fabre, records this interesting incident in one of his books. He spent many years observing and experimenting with 'processionary' caterpillars. They are called processionary because they attach themselves to one another to form a long train, moving around in that fashion most of the time. Each head snugly rests against the rump of its predecessor. Eyes-half closed, they move along as a unit, as the English saying goes, 'blind leading the blind.'

Jean Fabre once arranged a line of these caterpillars in a rotating ring by attaching the first caterpillar to the last so that the long procession did not have a beginning or an end. He then placed them in a very large flowerpot, keeping a close watch on them. Not too far away from the line food was also kept, so that if any of the caterpillars wished to eat, he could do so.

A week passed and to the surprise of Jean, the line was never broken. The caterpillars went on and on, till at last on the tenth day or so the ring halted, understandably of exhaustion and starvation. Linked together as a chain, they died together.

Anyone of the caterpillars could have stopped, instead of blindly following the others, at any time to eat and rest, as food was within reach. Anyone could have broken the line and led the others to safety. No one did. Instead, with their eyes half closed all continued their circular movement and perished together.

Points for Pro-Action

We are born to lead; but sometimes condemned to follow others blindly.

A wise person makes his/her own decisions; an ignorant person follows public opinion – Chinese proverb.

To choose to follow is to choose to destroy the leader in you.

It is easy to stand with the crowd; it takes courage to stand alone.

17

I Believe..!

'I believe in the sun even when it is not shining;

I believe in love even when I do not feel it;

I believe in God even when He is silent.'

These words on the wall of a concentration camp might have been surely written by one with a faith struggling in the darkness, in the apparent absence and silence of God. Gone are the person and the time; yet its lesson lasts longer that we wonder the quality of the person's faith.

Points for Pro-Action

Experience is not what happens to us but what we do with what happens to us.

Age wrinkles the body; but quitting wrinkles the soul.

There is no rainbow without little rain.

Every maze has an end.

18

I Failed Him; But He Trusted Me!

In World War I a fine lad in the battalion failed through illness in face of the enemy and was court-martialled and punished. Not wanting to let him down in his moment of despair, all that the colonel told his soldiers was, 'We must show him that we still trust him, or the lad will go to pieces.' Accordingly, not once did he allude to the unhappy incident; rather, he treated the boy with the old friendliness. A few weeks later, in a particularly tight corner, the colonel put the lad in command of the very company with whom he had been when he made his slip. In a few days' grim fighting the lad won honour after honour, and promotion for gallantry in the field. When asked about the magic, he confided to one of his friends, 'What else could I do? I failed him; but he trusted me.'

Points for Pro-Action

The best proof of love is trust.

The only way to make a person trustworthy is to trust the person.

Who we can trust largely depends upon who can trust us.

A faithful response to trust is bringing out the best out of oneself.

19

Beauty Is Indefinable!

There is a beautiful incident in Rabindranath Tagore's life. He used to go deep into the rivers in the lonely silences of the forest on his houseboat. One full moon night, he was on his houseboat reading a book on beauty by a great philosopher. His reading in candlelight enlightened him that the thoughts which were very deep on beauty made a deep impression in him. And he closed the book, concluding that beauty is indefinable. It was time for him to sleep and he blew out the candle. Suddenly from everywhere the moonlight came in dancing which had not so far entered through the windows of his cabin because of the candlelight.

He said, 'My God, what a fool I am. Beauty is standing at the door, almost knocking! I am blinded by a small candle, and I am so much absorbed in reading the book – which is nothing but empty words, which leads nowhere but into the desert of indefinability.

He opened all the windows, all the doors, and came out on the deck of the boat. He had seen many beautiful nights, many beautiful full moons, but he had never seen such beauty, such silence. On the river, it was all silver of the moon. He remained silent, almost moonstruck.

He wrote in his diary that night, 'The beauty can be seen, can be felt, can be experienced; it can drive you mad, but you cannot define it. And I decide from today not to read any book which an effort is to define beauty, because no book can do it.'

Points for Pro-Action

There is always more to see than what the eye meets.

Strangely sometimes, we are absent to the presence.

At times what prevents us from achieving awareness is what we think enlightens us.

Awareness empowers. But we are empowered only in proportion to our awareness.

20

Trifles Over Essentials!

The Buddha tells a story about freedom that goes something like this: A man is walking on a road through a wooded area. Suddenly he is struck down by an arrow. The arrow lodges in his chest. He is lying bleeding beside the road when another man comes along and attempts to help him. As the second man tries to remove the arrow without hurting the first man further, the wounded man struggles to sit up and says, 'Wait, wait…first tell me: did you see who shot the arrow? Which direction did it come from? Was the archer a Hindu, a Christian, a Buddhist, or a Muslim? Was the person male or female, rich or poor, friend or foe, progressive or conservative? Was it an accident, or was it deliberately aimed at me? What kind of punishment will the shooter receive after he dies? Do you believe in hell? And you – are you a believer? Does the arrow look like it's made of wood or of steel? Did you see anything – anything at all?' The second man says, 'What I can see is that you are in pain, that you are suffering, and that you will die if I can't remove this arrow. So please stop asking useless questions and let me help you.' He gives a yank on the arrow's shaft, and once it is removed the pain ceases – and so do the man's useless questions.

Points for Pro-Action

If we are engrossed with trifles, we deserve to miss out essentials.

Great minds discuss ideas; average minds discuss events; small minds discuss people – Eleanor Roosevelt.

Knowledge is power only if we have life.

We need to learn to put 'first things first.'

21

An Undeterred Journey in Love!

On July 12th, 2016 when Kashmir was in a state of turmoil and half the state was under curfew, a Kashmiri woman and her husband braved the strict curfew to get some food across to their Pandit friend. At first glance, Zubeda Begum and her husband walking on a deserted road in Srinagar with a bag of food items looked like any other desperate family trying to fend for itself in the strife-torn city. However, this couple was risking their lives to get some food to a friend, who had telephoned from across the river Jehlum to inform them of their plight. Following the curfew, the shops and establishments remained shut for days and there was no means of transport on the roads. To add to their woes, police limited the movement of people. When asked how they dared to risk, the woman said, 'She had called me in the morning saying her family needed food supplies. They have an ailing grandmother staying with them. I am taking the food to them. It is difficult, but we are trying to reach them.' Having an ailing grandmother at home, Diwanchand's family was desperately in need of help. 'Everyone is suffering here. We are so glad that these people came here. This is where humanity lies,' said Diwanchand Pandit. Curfew, violence, life threats, lack of food supplies, absence of transportation – nothing of these deterred their journey to reach their friends in need.

Points for Pro-Action

True love dares to transcend human-made boundaries like religion, creed, color, caste and what not!

The deepest love never says, 'give me,' but it does say, 'take.'

The more we love someone, the more we seek to give and the less we desire to receive.

Let us not be beggars of love but givers of it.

22

I Loved My Mother!

'I respected my father, but I loved my mother.' We should be taken aback by this statement because it is Adolf Hitler who has written these words of love for his mother in his autobiography *Mein Kampf*. Even the cruelest heart of Hitler had a tender feeling of love for his mother.

Points for Pro-Action

God could not be everywhere, and therefore He made mothers – A Jewish Proverb.

All that I am or hope to be, I owe to my angel mother – Abraham Lincoln.

A good mother is worth 100 schoolmasters.

If a child is God's gift, mother is God Himself as the gift.

23

The Package of a Call!

An Advertisement in a newspaper went like this: 'Men wanted for hazardous journey; small wages, bitter cold, long months of complete darkness, constant danger, safe return doubtful, honour and recognition in case of success.' On learning the demands of the call 5000 applicants came in. Of them just 28 were chosen for the Antarctic expedition in 1914 in a ship named 'Endurance'. As expected, the ship was crushed by heavy lumps of icebergs and all of them had to abandon the ship and floated in three small boats for 21 months. Eventually they accomplished the mission and reached the South Pole. All 28 returned victoriously.

Points for Pro-Action

Risks are a measure of people. People who won't make them are trying to preserve what they have. People who do take them often end up by having more.

Hesitation and delay are to be discouraged as non-values – Johann Lindworsky.

Those who lack courage will always find a philosophy to justify it – Albert Camus.

Purpose brings passion.

24

Che, Alive as They Never Wanted You To Be!

One of the greatest revolutionaries of the history Che Guevara was an Argentinean who was a key figure for the success of Cuban revolution. Wanting never to be stagnant he disowned ministerial positions in Cuba after some time and left for Congo and Bolivia where he finally met his end. He made his home where there was exploitation and injustice. He lost most of the wars he fought. But he became the most inspiring man like no other. Che once said, 'Failure does not necessarily mean that the cause you were fighting for was not worth it.' In the place where Che was executed, it has been written 'Che- alive, as they never wanted you to be!'

Points for Pro-Action

True love makes one a true rebel.

Because of a great love, one is courageous – Lao Tzu.

The ultimate measure of a person is not where the person stands in moments of comfort and convenience, but where he/she stands at times of challenge and controversy – Dr. Martin Luther King Jr.

Every one of us will die. But so, few of us really live.

25

The Herald Unseen!

Oseola Mccarthy was her name. She was born into poverty and therefore had to earn her living by doing the laundry. However, she was carefully saving every little amount of money till she was 87. One day when she went to the bank, the banker asked if she knew how much she had in her account and she nodded her head in negation. The banker himself said that she had saved a whopping Rs. 1,25,000,000 (over a quarter million dollars). Although she was not surprised, the banker was curious to know what she would do with that. She answered him that she would give the first part to the Church; three other parts to her nephews who took care of her all these years, and the rest to a special purpose without mentioning it. The next day she sent Rs. 75,00,000 to a local university for Poor Students Scholarship. She wanted other poor students to have the education that she could not dream of in her life. Before her death, her dream of seeing the first student who studied from her scholarship came true.

Points for Pro-Action

Only love can give meaning to something that on its own has none at all.

Contrary to liking, love demands nothing in return – Hugh Prather.

There is a saying: If you think you're too small to have an impact, try going to bed with a mosquito in the room.

Life is a story; make yours a bestseller.

26

United We Stand!

There is a legend about one of the decisive battles of Babur in 1526 to have a foothold in India. It was the battle of Panipat against Ibrahim Lodhi. Babur's army had just 8000 soldiers whereas Lodhi's army had 100000. Although Babur was about to use guns in that battle, the first ever man to have used guns in the subcontinent, yet he began to feel a bit foolish and foolhardy to engage with an army that was many times larger than his own. However, on the eve of this historic battle, Babur with a few of his generals and commanders went on a clandestine visit to spy over the hostile army from the top of a hillock. To his surprise, he found out that while having dinner, Lodhi's army was seated in different groups apart from one another. Besides this, the food served for various groups was different. Babur discovered that Lodhi's army was divided. Hence, he could foresee a victory with Lodhi. According to his expectations, Lodhi's divided army fell to the well-knit and united army of Babur.

Points for Pro-Action

Unity is the hallmark of real freedom.

It takes seven colours to form the rainbow.

The strength of the wolf is in the pack – Rudyard Kipling.

Let there be diversity not division.

27

I have Found Life So Beautiful!

Many of us might know Napoleon the Emperor of France. He had everything human persons would usually crave for; glory, power, riches etc. Yet towards the end of his life at the island of St. Helena he said, 'I have never known six happy days in my life.' Similarly, we might also know Helen Keller, the celebrated lady of America who went deaf and blind after 19 months from her birth. She had everything that the world considered a curse. Still she happened to say at the end of her life that 'I have found life so beautiful.'

Points for Pro-Action

Our greatest ability is the power to choose.

Let us realize that there are no hopeless situations; there are only people who take hopeless attitudes.

Attitudes are more important than facts.

If we are rich in attitude, we will find the glass half-full and not half-empty.

28

With Malice Toward None!

Abraham Lincoln the notable president in the history of America was re-elected as his first term was over. Meanwhile he had so much to hate others because his own people reacted strongly with a rebellion for his Emancipation Proclamation. Once his stint as a president was over, many of his enemies plotted for his failure. Still, people loved him so much that he was offered to take on the mantle for the second time. All his enemies least expected this turn of history and therefore began to feel intimidated by his succession. To the contrary, Abraham Lincoln spoke at his second inauguration the most beautiful and noble phrases ever uttered by a ruler of men.

'With malice toward none

With charity for all.'

Points for Pro-Action

To err is human; to forgive is divine.

Forgiveness is the willingness to begin; guilt is the love of staying stuck – Hugh Prather.

Forgiveness is a great act of spirit and personal courage. It is also one of the best ways to elevate the quality of your life – Robin Sharma.

There can be no progress without forgiveness. Chewing the bitter cud of revenge and guilt signals one's stagnation.

29

Love of Enemies!

When the American troops captured the concentration camps after the World War II, three young Hungarian Jews hid one SS commander of Nazi and released him on condition of no pain and torture. It was because he was so kind to them that he paid no small amount of money from his own pocket in order to purchase medicines for his prisoners. He distributed them clothes collected from Bavarian villages because what they had were inherited from other inmates of the camp who were gassed to death.

Points for Pro-Action

I destroy my enemies when I make them my friends – Abraham Lincoln.

A prayer: 'God! Protect me from my betrayers; I will take care of my enemies.'

It is difficult to love our enemies. Much simpler not to have enemies at all!

An open enemy is better than a false friend.

30

I Can Turn the Night Into Day!

There is a cruel legend about Emperor Nadir Shah who was infamous for his brutality of oppressing and killing people. Once when he attacked India, he ordered his soldiers to bring the most beautiful woman of the locality to engage him with her songs and dance. The woman came and indeed made a gift of her ability to sing and dance that Nadir Shah became very happy and hence he rewarded her with ornaments and jewels of priceless value. While it was time for her to depart, she refused to go in the dark with so much valuables with her. On learning her fear, he commanded his soldiers, 'You go ahead of her, and go on burning everything that you find – forest, village, anything. Make it a light.' And he told the woman, 'Now you can go. And you will remember that you had come to see the great Emperor Nadir Shah who can turn the night into day.' It is said, on that single night he burnt seven villages and the whole forest to make it almost look like day.

Points for Pro-Action

Subjects become playthings in the hands of cruel rulers.

It is much more secure to be feared than to be loved – Niccolo Machiavelli.

Kings are in the moral order what monsters are in the natural – Henri Gregoire.

When God wants to a judge a nation, He gives them wicked rulers.

31

The Praying Hands!

Back in the fifteenth century, in a tiny village near Nuremberg, lived a family with eighteen children. Eighteen! In order merely to keep food on the table for this mob, the father and head of the household, a goldsmith by profession, worked almost eighteen hours a day at his trade and any other paying chore he could find in the neighbourhood. Despite their seemingly hopeless condition, two of Albrecht Durer the Elder's children had a dream. They both wanted to pursue their talent for art, but they knew full well that their father would never be financially able to send either of them to Nuremberg to study at the Academy.

After many long discussions at night in their crowded bed, the two boys finally worked out a pact. They would toss a coin. The loser would go down into the nearby mines and, with his earnings, support his brother while he attended the academy. Then, when that brother who won the toss completed his studies, in four years, he would support the other brother at the academy, either with sales of his artwork or, if necessary, also by labouring in the mines.

They tossed a coin on a Sunday morning after church. Albrecht Durer won the toss and went off to Nuremberg. Albert went down into the dangerous mines and, for the next four years, financed his brother, whose work at the academy was almost an immediate sensation. Albrecht's etchings, his woodcuts, and his oils were far better than those of most of his professors, and by the time he graduated, he was beginning to earn considerable fees for his commissioned works.

When the young artist returned to his village, the Durer family held a festive dinner on their lawn to celebrate Albrecht's triumphant homecoming. After a long and memorable meal, punctuated with music and laughter, Albrecht rose from his honoured position at the head of the table to drink a toast to his beloved brother for the years of sacrifice that had enabled Albrecht to fulfil his ambition. His closing words were, 'And now, Albert, blessed brother of mine, now it is your turn. Now you can go to Nuremberg to pursue your dream, and I will take care of you.'

All heads turned in eager expectation to the far end of the table where Albert sat, tears streaming down his pale face, shaking his lowered head from side to side while he sobbed and repeated, over and over, 'No ... no ...no ...no.'

Finally, Albert rose and wiped the tears from his cheeks. He glanced down the long table at the faces he loved, and then, holding his hands close to his right cheek, he said softly, 'No, brother. I cannot go to Nuremberg. It is too late for me. Look ... look what four years in the mines have done to my hands! The bones in every finger have been smashed at least once, and lately, I have been suffering from arthritis so badly in my right hand that I cannot even hold a glass to return your toast, much less make delicate lines on parchment or canvas with a pen or a brush. No, brother ... for me, it is too late.'

Feeling sad and crestfallen for what had befallen his beloved brother on account of his sacrifice, to pay homage to Albert for all his sacrifices, Albrecht Durer painstakingly drew his brother's abused hands with palms together and thin fingers stretched skyward. He called his powerful drawing simply 'Hands,' but the entire world almost immediately opened their hearts to his great masterpiece and renamed his tribute of love 'The Praying Hands.'

Points for Pro-Action

No one ever makes it alone!

It takes two hands for a clap.

Behind every tale of success, there are scores of diminished lives.

A success is nothing but the result of a score of sacrifices.

32

Education of The Heart!

At the entrance of an educational institute the following message was posted for contemplation:

'Destroying any nation does not require the use of atomic bombs or the use of long range missiles.

It only requires lowering the quality of education and allowing cheating in the examinations by the students.

Patients die at the hands of such doctors.

Buildings collapse at the hands of such engineers.

Money is lost at the hands of such economists & accountants.

Humanity dies at the hands of such religious scholars.

Justice is lost at the hands of such judges.

The collapse of education is the collapse of the nation.'

Points for Pro-Action

Real education is education of the heart.

Education refines the mind; purifies the heart; ennobles the character.

Education enables the person to turn one's shadows into light.

Education is about getting introduced to the culture of truth and civility.

33

The Real Cost of Vanity!

Nasiruddin appeared at court wearing a magnificent turban and asking for money for charity. 'You come here asking for money and yet you are wearing an extremely expensive turban on your head. How much did that extraordinary thing cost?' asked the sultan. 'It was a gift from someone very rich. And it's worth, I believe, five hundred gold coins,' replied the wise Sufi. The sultan's minister muttered: 'That's impossible. No turban could possibly be worth that much.' Nasiruddin insisted: 'I didn't come here only to beg, I also came to do business, I know that only a true sovereign would be capable of buying this turban for six hundred gold coins so that I could give the surplus to the poor.' The sultan was flattered and paid what Nasiruddin asked. On the way out, Nasiruddin said to the minister: 'You may know the value of a turban, but I know how far a man's vanity will take him.'

Points for Pro-Action

Vanity is the flatterer of the soul – Edward Counsel.

Reason ends where vanity begins.

Vanity surfaces when people forget who they are and start believing what others speak of them.

Vanity is the world of the super class, everyone's dream, a world without shadows or darkness, where 'yes' is the only possible answer to any request – Paulo Coelho.

34

Heart Brothers!

Sometime ago, a film called '*Ahim Balev*' (Heart Brothers) telling the story of a heart transplant from a 19 year old Israeli Jewish soldier to an Arab recipient grabbed much attention. It was an example of how biotechnology can come to the aid, not only of saving a life, but also of overcoming deep-rooted mistrust and bridging the relationships between communities. 'I am standing there in the operating room, there's a moment when I'm holding the Jewish heart in one hand and the Arab heart in the other, and I look down and suddenly it occurs to me, there's no difference between them.' These words of Dr Jacob Lavee, Cardiac Surgeon and Director of the Department of transplantation at the Sheba Medical Centre in Israel who conducted this heart transplant show how organ transplant can be an occasion to recognize the common brotherhood of all human beings.

Points for Pro-Action

Every act of enmity with others is a revelation of enmity within oneself.

Often, the barriers that we speak of pertain to the inside of a person.

Let us not rush to condemn the other as one in fault because we are all bad in someone's story.

At the base of enmity lies insecurity; with freedom is born real love.

35

Discovering Oneself in Service!

D r. Garth Alfred Taylor was born in Montego Bay, Jamaica, in 1944. He was a gifted eye surgeon, a family man and above all else – a humanitarian. One of his favourite sayings was: 'I came into this world with nothing, and all I'm going to leave with is my conscience.' He gave life to his words. What made Garth's impact so profound was that he didn't just practice medicine – he lived it. For more than 20 years, he travelled around the world, to developing nations, selflessly helping to save people's sight. In his own words, 'I found my nirvana 23 years ago....by treating avoidable blindness. People don't just get back their sight, they get back their self-esteem.' Because he cared and had the courage to act, he blessed the lives of thousands of people. At his funeral, the church was so full that many people had to stand out on the street.

Points for Pro-Action

Either write something worth reading or do something worth writing – Benjamin Franklin.

Service to humankind is service to God – MK Gandhi.

Service to others is the rent you pay for your room here on earth – Muhammad Ali.

Only a life lived for others is a life worthwhile – Albert Einstein.

36

Hope – The Greatest Possession of All!

It is recorded of Alexander the Great that when he succeeded to the throne of Macedon, he gave away amongst his friends the greater part of the estates which his father had left him. When Perdiccas asked him what he restored for himself Alexander answered – 'The greatest possession of all – Hope.'

Points for Pro-Action

To hope is to rest assured about blessings of the future.

Our courage doubles with hope and halved by doubt and fear.

Be sure! You can lose anything but not hope!

Hope can insulate us against any negativity that can paralyse our spirit.

37

The Name Mandela Gave!

Nelson Mandela was imprisoned at Robben Island. Once when his grandchild was given to him to be named, he gave her a name that would symbolize the struggle of South Africans against the imposed discrimination under apartheid. His granddaughter would be called Zaziwe – hope. He recounted later saying, 'The name had a special meaning for me, for during all my years in prison hope never left me – and now it never would. I was convinced that this child would be a part of a new generation of South Africans for whom apartheid would be a distant memory – that was my dream.'

Points for Pro-Action

Giving hope is the most needed humanitarian service that we can render the society.

Economic prosperity has not guaranteed simultaneous increase of happiness and Joy; the result is more insecurity, uncertainty and despair.

Hope not only abolishes the feeling of insecurity; but prepares us for the better.

Hope is the antidote to all ills that ail humanity.

38

But What Is Nirvana?

Buddha was asked by his puzzled disciples, 'But what is Nirvana? For sometimes you speak of it as if it were a present thing, and sometimes as if it lay in the future.' He replied, 'It is both. It is the ideal: is present because it begins here; and future, because after death it expands into a far greater being that what we can know now can be translated into the best that is conceivable.'

Points for Pro-Action

Giving life to the divine in us is the ultimate spiritual wisdom.

We don't know how heaven really looks like; but if we can change this world into a better place, then it is well here on earth.

Earthly life is brief time of preparation for what we might face after death.

It is important to be the change we want to see in the world.

Delights To Cherish

39

He Led from The Front!

The entire world came to know of Luiz Urzua through the tragic Chilean mine accident that took place on 5 August 2010. The heroic rescue of 33 Chilean miners, trapped for 69 days 2,000 feet below the ground started and the entire world looked glued to the rescue operation. For the shift foreman Luiz Urzua (the leader), the challenges began within moments of the mine collapse.

According to a navy rescue commander, 'For a miner, their shift leader is sacred and holy. They would never think about replacing him. That is carved in stone; it is one of the commandments in the life of a miner.' The role of Urzua at the point of crisis was such that he quickly ordered his men to huddle while he took three miners and scouted up the tunnel, searching for information on the massive cave-in.

Correctly deducing that the men were trapped, Urzua instituted a set of rules and regulations that were both methodically rigid and crucial to the men's survival. He ordered that the mine's stash of emergency food be rationed into minimal portions – two spoonfuls of tuna fish and half a glass of milk every 48 hours. It was his foresight and crucial decision-making that kept the Chilean miners alive for two months. That was also his secret for keeping the men bonded and focussed on survival.

Although he was the leader, the leading of the team was done by majority decision-making. Like a ship's captain, 54-year-old Urzúa was the last to leave the cave after 70 days of trap below the Atacama Desert. Although the entire world hailed those miners as models of solidarity, the truth was not so simple. There was the waiting for death, the hopelessness, the petty squabbles and the nagging and the unspoken fear of cannibalism. As shift boss Luis Urzua managed to overcome darkness, despair and the prospect of starvation to mobilize a team, who worked together to ensure that every man survived and thrived in the worst of conditions. He was able to oversee, organize, protect, and tend to the emotional needs of the 33 men trapped in the mine in Chile.

Chile's President said to Luis Urzua: 'You acted like a good boss.' Great leaders are able to inspire by adhering to what Sinek calls 'the golden circle' - you start with why and move to how. And Luiz Urzua did that.

Points for Pro-Action

Readiness to lead implies readiness to sacrifice.

Vision is the eyesight of a leader.

Leadership is not about the honour one receives but about the responsibility ahead.

Real leadership is just the extended understanding of being a servant.

40

Turning Scars into Stars!

Viktor Frankl, an eminent Jewish psychiatrist, was standing naked and stripped before the Gestapo. They had taken his watch, then had seen his gold wedding band, and demanded it as well. As Frankl took wedding band off his finger to hand it to the Gestapo officer, a thought went through his brain. *'There is one thing that you can never take from me and that is my freedom to choose how I will react to whatever you do to me!'*

Points for Pro-Action

If you choose to react positively, not negatively, to the hurts of life, you can turn your scars into stars – Robert Schuller.

Pain is inevitable. Suffering is optional – Haruki Murakami.

What we choose often decides who we become.

When the future looks bleak, positivity looks for a fresh beginning and for ray of hope.

41

The Life of A Traitor!

Benedict Arnold, during the American War of Independence, sold military secrets to the British. His countrymen discovered the plot, but Arnold managed to escape to England because his existence in America would not be possible. However, once he was in England, people did not want to speak to him, or to be seen around with him. He was grossly insulted in public places. It is said that some people spat on his face. Wherever he went, his reputation as a traitor followed him. He was always known as 'Benedict Arnold, the Traitor.'

Points for Pro-Action

Traitors are hated even by those whom they prefer – Tacitus.

The saddest thing about betrayal is that it is never from enemies but from friends and loved ones.

Betrayal is always done against love, loyalty and trust.

A traitor is still a traitor even if he befriends us.

42

I Would Ask for Tomorrow!

A big battle was building for the morning. The place was Korea, the hour midnight. It was bitter cold, the temperature below zero. A burly U.S. marine was leaning against a tank eating cold beans out of a can with a penknife. A newspaper correspondent watching him was moved to propound a philosophical question: 'Look' he said, 'If I were God and could give you what you wanted most, what would you ask for?' The marine dug out another penknife of beans, thought reflectively, then said, 'I would ask for tomorrow.'

Points for Pro-Action

Sometimes our hearts long for what we miss badly.

When life looks so uncertain for a soldier, his only desire may be to look for one more day.

The true soldier fights not because he hates what is in front of him, but because he loves what is behind him – G.K. Chesterton.

Days of danger and nights of waking is what the soldiers are prized for the choice of serving their motherland.

Dig It Out Again!

Workmen building the Panama Canal were digging and excavating the big ditch for a long time. Just as they thought it was finished, there was a huge landslide and much of the dirt taken out fell back in again. The man in charge dashed up to the boss, General Goethals, and exclaimed: 'It's terrible! Terrible! All the dirt's back in again! What shall we do?' Goethals said calmly, 'Dig it out again.' What else was there to do?

Points for Pro-Action

There are no shortcuts to any place worth going – Beverly Sills.

The best way is always through.

To conquer frustration, one must remain intensely focused on the outcome, not the obstacles – T.F. Hodge.

Challenges are what make like interesting; overcoming them is what makes life meaningful.

44

If Only He Had Persisted!

There's a story about a rusty pickaxe found in the old Colorado gold country. The handle had long since deteriorated, but the rusted pick remained driven into the ground a hundred years or more. The way it was driven hard into the earth revealed the defeat felt by some frustrated prospector. It seemed to say: 'Oh, what is the use? I'm through. The pathetic fact – which this unknown defeated prospector never learned – was that a few yards farther on was a rich vein of gold which later produced millions. If only he had persisted!

Points for Pro-Action

Persistence is when we don't submit to discouragements, frustrations and despair.

Persistence is to the character of man as carbon is to steel – Napoleon Hill.

Winners never quit, and quitters never win.

Never give up! You never know how close you may be to achieving your dreams.

45

Anger Destroys Everything!

One morning, the Mongol warrior, Genghis Khan, and his court went out hunting. His companions carried bows and arrows, but Genghis Khan carried on his arm his favourite falcon, which was better and surer than any arrow, because it could fly up into the skies and see everything that a human being could not.

However, despite the group's enthusiastic efforts, they found nothing. Disappointed, Genghis Khan returned to the encampment and in order not to take out his frustration on his companions, he left the rest of the party and rode on alone. They had stayed in the forest any longer than expected, and Khan was desperately tired and thirsty. In the summer heat, all the streams had dried up, and he could find nothing to drink. Then, to his amazement, he saw a thread of water flowing from a rock just in front of him.

He removed the falcon from his arm and took out the silver cup which he always carried with him. It was very slow to fill and, just as he was about to raise it to his lips, the falcon flew up, plucked the cup from his hands, and dashed it to the ground.

Genghis Khan was furious, but then the falcon was his favourite, and perhaps it, too, was thirsty. He picked up the cup, cleaned off the dirt, and filled it again. When the cup was only half-empty this time, the falcon again attacked it, spilling the water.

Genghis Khan adored this bird, but he knew that he could not, under any circumstances, allow such disrespect; someone might be watching this scene from afar and, later, would tell his warriors that the great conqueror incapable of taming a mere bird.

This time, he drew his sword, picked up the cup and refilled it, keeping one eye on the stream and the other on the falcon. As soon as he had enough water in the cup and was ready to drink, the falcon again took flight and flew towards him. Khan, with one thrust, pierced the bird's breast.

The thread of water, however, had dried up; but Khan, determined now to find something to drink, climbed the rock in search of the spring. To his surprise, there really was a pool of water and, in the middle of it, dead, lay one of the most poisonous snakes in the region. If he had drunk the water, he, too, would have died.

Khan returned to camp with the dead falcon in his arms. He ordered a gold figurine of the bird to be made and on one of the wings, he had engraved: 'Even when a friend does something you do not like, he continues to be your friend.' And on the other wing, he had these words engraved: 'Any action committed in anger is an action doomed to failure.'

Points for Pro-Action

Don't do something permanently hurtful, just because you are temporarily angry.

When consumed by hatred, we perceive enemies everywhere.

When love wanes, even petty mistakes loom large into punishable offences.

Just because you are angry doesn't mean that you have the right to be cruel.

46

True Sportsmanship!

At the first Grand Slam tennis event of 2009, the Australian Open, one got to see sublime tennis as well as the depth of the human soul in the final that pitted Rafael Nadal against Roger Federer. For the record, Federer lost a classic to Nadal; the match went the complete five-set distance and will, undoubtedly, be a manual for aspiring tennis players the world over. The behaviour of the two champions at the presentation ceremony after the match, however, should speak to the heart of every human being.

As Federer, carrying his runner-up shield, choked on his tears, the pain on the face of Nadal was there for all to see. The latter's body language as he accepted the champion's trophy, was muted. There have been many poignant and moving spectacles of triumph in sports. That Sunday afternoon at the Rod Laver arena in Melbourne the stage expanded to show us the greatness of the human spirit. Here then were two men, joining not just by sporting history, but by mutual recognition of the effort it has taken to mould themselves into the champions they are. They know only too well the hours of grinding, pounding training that make their route, day after day.

These are two men who recognize that behind every champion stand many shadows mocking their passion and ability. These are two men joined by deep respect for each other's pain and talent. Boxer Muhammad Ali once said, 'Champions are made from something they have deep inside them – a desire, a dream, a vision.' Nadal and Federer are two champions who on that stage showed their essential connectedness.

Their rivalry is already being hailed as one of the greatest ever in the game, but that did not stop Federer from weeping openly at his loss. He was not afraid to show his wound to his great rival, to tell him all his sacrifices in preparing for the tournament had come to naught. He did not keep a brave face. Sans ego, the vulnerable Federer touched a chord in all of us. Nadal not only saw the wound, he felt it.

A saying goes thus: 'Just as the fruit-laden tree bows low, so does the accomplished person in humility.' Never has one heard of a champion apologizing to the defeated rival for his win. Nadal has done that on several occasions. He said sorry to Federer at the post-match press conference and immediately after collecting the championship trophy from Rod Laver. The winner of the Australian Open though young, had the humility of the truly wise.

Points for Pro-Action

Good players inspire themselves; great players inspire others.

Win as if you were used to it; lose as if you enjoyed it for a change – Ralph Waldo Emerson.

In any sport, we don't compete against our opponents; but ourselves.

It is striving to outdo our previous performance that qualifies sportsmanship.

Refining the Human Mind!

As a child Alexander Dumas was walking along the road when he saw pieces of a broken mirror. He picked up the largest piece and started playing with it. He discovered that he could reflect light into caves, tunnels and dark crevices where light could not enter. It occurred to him that the best way to refine the human mind is to reflect light to make it bright. With this insight, he started writing books to help uplift the human mind to reach heights – all through its own efforts.

Points for Pro-Action

A book is a dream that you hold in your hands.

Every book is a spiritual pharmacy.

Books are basically thoughts frozen in print.

Reading is by far the most successful pursuit of happiness.

The Art of Slowing Down!

While inspiration can come to anyone at any time, you can create a conducive climate within you so that you get self-inspired. For self-inspiration, both your heart and mind need to be relaxed, so that you are in leisure mode. Isaac Newton was relaxing in the garden when he saw an apple fall. He had the leisure to ask himself why the apple fell straight on the ground and did not go upward. He found the answer and propounded the law of gravity.

Points for Pro-Action

Unfortunately, pace has become synonymous with progress in our age.

Are we aware of the art of slowing down?

Do we take time to stand and stare?

Beyond all doubts, relaxation is the key to newness.

49

A Bullock-Cart Flying!

A small airplane was left in the jungles of Burma when Japan was defeated; the Japanese left it there. The aboriginals who lived in the forest found it. They were very curious, excited – what is it? But seeing the wheels… they figured out that it is a kind of bullock cart, but some idiotic people have made it because this is not the way bullock carts are made. They started using that airplane, small airplane, as a bullock cart. Just by chance a man, a hunter, saw them: he could not believe his eyes – an airplane being used as a bullock cart!

He asked them, 'Have you made it? They said, 'No, we are not such idiots, why should we make it? We have found it. But we are enjoying it.' The hunter was from a nearby village where he had seen buses, cars. He said, 'It seems to be a kind of car. It is not a bullock cart. You just wait; I will bring one of my friends who knows something about buses.' He used to work for a bus transport service. So, they brought some petrol, and it did work like a small bus. And the people thought it was hilarious. They said, 'so we were wrong, it is not a bullock cart; it is a bus. Great idea! They enjoyed it.

And then the mechanic who had come said, 'I don't know much about airplanes, but as far as I can see it is not a bus. I have seen airplanes only in the air. My village is small. Buses come up to my village and I have worked on the buses, so I can help with this airplane – but this is an airplane because you can see the wings. I know a man in the city – I will find him, and I will bring him – who knows about airplanes.'

And the man from the city came and he said, 'What nonsense is this? You are using a beautiful airplane as a bus, and that too in the jungle where there is no road, nothing. You are just dragging it through muddy roads. It can fly.' The aboriginals said, 'It can fly? Is it a bird? He said, 'It is a bird – have you not seen steel birds flying?' They said, 'We have seen, but we have never seen them on the earth.'

The man managed…he took a few aboriginals with him and the airplane functioned as it was supposed to function – it started flying. And the whole village was dancing, beating their drums, singing, 'This is great! A bullock cart flying!'

Points for Pro-Action

If we don't know who we are and what we are capable of, we may not realize the full potential of ourselves.

Success begins with the realistic appraisal of oneself.

In our ignorance, we are very much like the elephants shackled by a tiny chain which they knew from childhood they cannot break.

There goes a saying: 'What I am today' sadly looks at 'who I should have been.'

50

A Daring Vocation!

On June 8, 2017 a boy by name Varshil from Gujarat hit the headlines of dailies and adorned the cover features of magazines. A 99.9 percentile in Class 12 is a ticket to top-flight colleges and a lucrative career. For that boy of a middle-class origin, it was a dream come true. Everyone thought that the boy would make the most out of it. However, he chose a different path. He renounced the world to become a Jain monk. As of now the boy had embraced the hardest life imaginable. The Jain monks walk barefoot, wear only white cotton cloth, and eat just one meal a day. They are not allowed to take bath – this is to safeguard the life forms in the water. At the most they can sponge themselves using boiled water. It is a life of hardship, to cut the long story short.

Points for Pro-Action

If you have not learnt to sacrifice for what you desire to achieve, what you desire becomes the sacrifice.

Our movement forward should be a simultaneous disowning of what pulls us behind.

The rolling stone gathers no mass.

If only we are found in constant advance movement, we can leave behind all that cause our stagnation.

51

We Just Add A New Lamb Everyday!

A visitor went to a zoo and was surprised to notice a lion and a sheep sitting quietly in a single cell. This coexistence surprised him more than ever because he had never witnessed it anywhere in his life. Finding it hard to restrain himself from asking, he went to the zoo director and exclaimed how such coexistence of lion and sheep was possible despite remaining in a single cell. Maintaining his nonchalant composure, the director just commented – 'we just add a new lamb every day.'

Points for Pro-Action

Peace descends not with compromises but with reconciliation.

All that glitters is not gold.

Peace is an internal quality but unfortunately sought very much outside.

Peace is not merely an absence of conflict; it is ensuring the common good.

52

Every Knot Shortens the Thread!

'Rabbi', the disciples said, 'why do you teach that God is closer to sinners than to the perfect ones?' 'Well', the old rabbi explained, 'every time we sin, we break the thread that ties us to God. Every time we repent, God ties it up again. And every knot shortens the thread.' Now, isn't that a lovely thought? It is the weakness of the soul that brings us always closer to God, not its perfectionism.

Points for Pro-Action

Those who have never known guilt have never known their own best selves.

Healthy guilt is neither scrupulosity nor rationalization. It simply looks personal failure in the eye and says, 'I can do better than that.'

If we can still feel moral angst, we can feel everything else in life, too.

Self-righteousness is a disservice.

53

I Am Ever Present with Her!

In a village there was an elderly couple, well-advanced in age that the old lady became blind and it was her husband who took care of her. The old man worked hard in order that he could run the family with the meager income he earned from agriculture. However, their daily life was marked by a strange behavior. The neighbors noticed that the old man was always whistling whenever he was far away from home working in the fields. Unable to restrain their curiosity, once they dared to ask the old man about his peculiar act of whistling. He replied, 'My wife is blind and therefore cannot see me working in the field. Whenever she does not hear from me, she grows little anxious as to think what had happened to me. In order to reassure her of my presence, I whistle from time to time and she also understands that I am not far away from her. It is my language to speak to her that I am ever present with her.'

Points for Pro-Action

In real love, the other person takes precedence than the self.

'I am with you' is a powerful assurance of nearness.

Love is identifying one with the other in all the ways possible.

When we really care for someone, their happiness matters more than ours.

54

Myth of Icarus!

There is an interesting Greek mythology. Icarus was the son of the master craftsman Daedalus, the creator of the labyrinth. In order that he should not reveal the secret of creating the labyrinth, the king of Crete imprisoned Daedalus and his son Icarus. However, both father and son attempted to escape from Crete by means of the wings Daedalus made from feathers and wax. Before flight, Daedalus warned his son Icarus first of complacency and then of hubris, instructing him that he should neither fly too high nor too low, so the sun's heat would not melt them or the sea's dampness would not clog his wings respectively. Icarus ignored his father's instructions and took joy and pride in flying too close to the sun only to get drowned in the sea when the wax in his wings got melted by the hot sun and therefore tumbled out of the sky.

Points for Pro-Action

Obedience is the mother of success and is wedded to safety – Aeschylus.

True learning takes place in an atmosphere of trust and openness to the mentor.

Obedience is the first step to climb the ladder of success and greatness.

A soul that is humble at learning, thrives in commanding.

55

Life Is Beautiful!

The movie *Life is Beautiful* is a splendid portrayal of a father's struggle to save his son from negativities he might have to face in life due to dehumanizing social and political realities. Basically, the movie is about a father who tries to shelter his innocent son from the ugliness of the world, no matter how ugly the world might be. Therefore, the movie is not about Nazis and Fascists, but about the human spirit that dares to laugh in the face of the unthinkable.

Guido has a Jewish background, and when he and his son are sent to a concentration camp, he does his best to keep his son (Giosue) from finding out the brutal truth of their situation. He mostly does this by telling him they are playing a game. The father in the movie instructs his son that he cannot cry, ask for his mother or declare he's hungry; lest only to result in the loss of the 'game,' in other words - death. However, in the end to save his son from the tyranny of death, the father jeopardises his own survival thus preventing the Germans from discovering Giosue. The Americans break into the seemingly deserted camp the following morning. Giosue emerges just as a tank pulls around the corner. Hitching a lift out, Giosué soon spots his mother and the film closes.

Points for Pro-Action

Life is robbed off its charm because we tend to think of it in terms of failures, uncertainties and disappointments.

From a realistic point of view, life has its own lessons through pain, misfortune and misery notwithstanding the fact of blessings, love and peace it offers.

At times, we are weighed down so much by the miseries we face forgetting really the blessings we need to count.

It is so unfortunate that a dot clouds the vision that we hardly see the white sheet but the little black dot.

56

They Are Trying to Promote Me!

'The reason the king is so powerful is because he has made a pact with the devil,' a very devout woman in the street told the boy, and he was intrigued. Sometime later, when he was travelling to another town, the boy heard a man beside him remark: 'All this land belongs to the same man. I would say the Devil had a hand in that.' Late one summer afternoon, a beautiful woman walked past the boy. 'That woman is in the service of Satan!' cried a preacher angrily. From then on, the boy decided to seek the Devil out, and when he found him, he said: 'They say you can make people powerful, rich, and beautiful.' 'Not really,' replied the Devil. 'You have just been listening to the views of those who are trying to promote me.'

Points for Pro-Action

Badness is the point at which we cease to care what effect our own actions will have on others.

What is goodness? It is the person in your life who surprised you with virtue at a time when evil would have been understandable.

Most of the evil in this world is done by people with good intentions – T.S. Eliot.

Unknowingly, in judging others, we are often judging ourselves.

57

The One Among You!

In a time of great war and consternation, there was a monastery that had fallen upon hard times. There were few monks left, and they tended to squabble among themselves. Everyone was convinced that their path was right, and the peaceful ways of the past seemed like more than a dream. In a last attempt to save the monastery, the Abbott sought the advice of an old rabbi, who was reputed to have immense wisdom and insight into the workings of humanity. When the Abbott told the rabbi of the situation, he shook his head in great concern. 'It is imperative that you find a way to resolve this situation before it is too late,' said the rabbi. 'For what you don't realise is that among you is the one who will deliver you all from fear into love.'

The Abbott asked who among them was the one, but the rabbi would tell him no more. On the way back to the monastery, he wondered who the one could be. 'I bet it is Brother Arthur,' he thought to himself. 'He is kind and good. Or perhaps it is Brother Thomas – he is young but already shows great wisdom. Or could it be...no...I must not even consider that it might be me!' On his return, the abbot shared the news with the monks. Although they were startled, there was a ring of truth to what he had said. The one was among them!

As they contemplated which of them it might be, the monks began to treat one another with a very special reverence and respect. After all, someone among them might really be the one. Similarly, each monk thinking that himself might be the one, they began to treat themselves with extraordinary respect and reverence as well.

As time went by, the monks developed a gentle, loving quality, which was hard to quantify but easy to notice. They lived respectfully, in harmony with themselves and nature. An aura of peace and reverence seemed to radiate out from them and permeate the atmosphere. There was something strangely attractive, even compelling about it. Before long, people were coming from far and wide to be nourished by the life of the monks, and young men were asking to become part of their community.

Within a few short years, the monastery had once again become home to a thriving order – a vibrant centre of light and spirituality in the world.

Points for Pro-Action

We come to know God only through our neighbours.

Holiness begins with respecting the other in their dignity.

The self cannot exist, cannot have a concept of itself as self, without the other – Emmanuel Levinas.

I don't judge people by the scriptures of their faith or the scars from their past; I embrace them by the content of their hearts – Dodinsky.

58

Master of Happiness!

A master of happiness was travelling with a cumbersome bag upon his shoulder when he came across a seeker. The seeker asked him what true happiness really felt like. The master paused for a moment, then smiled and took the bag off his shoulder. As it dropped heavily to the ground, he stood tall in the freedom from the burden he had been carrying. The seeker said, 'I think I understand. And what do you do once you are happy?' The master smiled, hoisted his bag, and carried on down the road.

Points for Pro-Action

Burden is not when carrying but when we have nothing to carry; nothing to contribute; nothing to do.

There is a joy in doing more; in doing better.

Life unencumbered by responsibilities may look appealing. But it is a burden.

To be of some use to oneself, to others and to the world is a blessing indeed.

59

The Story of The Two Jewels!

A very devout rabbi lived happily with his family – an admirable wife and their two beloved sons. Once, because of his work, the rabbi had to be away from home for several days. During that period, both children were killed in a terrible car accident. Alone, the mother suffered in silence. However, because she was a strong woman, sustained by faith and trust in God, she endured the shock with dignity and courage. But how was she to break the tragic news to her husband? His faith was equally strong, but he had, in the past, been taken into hospital with heart problems, and his wife feared that finding out about the tragedy might cause his death too. All she could do was to pray to God to advise her on the best way to act.

On the eve of her husband's return, she prayed hard and was granted the grace of an answer. The following day, the rabbi arrived home, embraced his wife, and asked after the children. The woman told him not to worry about them now, but to take a bath and rest. Sometime later, they sat down to lunch. She asked him all about his trip, and he told her everything that had happened to him; he spoke about God's mercy, and then again asked about the children. The wife, somewhat awkwardly, replied: 'Don't worry about the children. We will deal with them later. First, I need your help to solve what I consider to be a very grave problem.' Her husband asked anxiously: 'What has happened? I thought you looked distressed. Tell me everything that is on your mind, and I am sure that, with God's help, we can solve any problem together.'

'While you were away, a friend of ours visited us and left two jewels of incalculable value here for me to look after. They are lovely jewels!

I have never seen anything so beautiful before. He has since come to claim them back, and I don't want to return them. I have grown too fond of them. What should I do?' 'I can't understand your behaviour at all! You have never been a woman given to vanity!' 'It is just that I have never seen such jewels before! I can't bear the idea of losing them forever.' And the rabbi said firmly: 'No one can lose something he or she has not possessed. Keeping those jewels would be tantamount to stealing them. We will give them back, and I will help you make up for their loss. We will do this together today.' 'As you wish, my love. The treasures will be returned. In fact, they already have been. The two precious jewels were our sons. God entrusted them to our care, and while you were away, he came to fetch them back. They have gone.' The rabbi understood. He embraced his wife, and together they wept many tears; but he had understood the massage and, from that day on, they struggled to bear the loss together.

Points for Pro-Action

A part of us dies with the death of our beloved ones as well.

Grief is about loss – especially the loss is of something or someone we cannot get back.

The beauty of life is this: joy when shared with others is doubled; but pain when shared with others is halved.

Compassion is to share the pain without sharing the suffering – Shinzen Young.

60

To Me You Have Given Yourself!

L ong ago, a wise and good king ruled in Persia. He loved his people and wanted to know how they lived. He wanted to know about their hardships. So, he dressed himself in the clothes of a peasant and went to the homes of the poor. No one whom he visited suspected that he was their king. One of them was a very poor man who lived in a cellar. The king ate his coarse food with him and cheered him up. Then he left. Later he visited the poor man again and disclosed his identity. The king thought the man would ask for some gift or favour, but he didn't. Instead he said, 'You left your palace and your glory to visit me in this dark, dreary place. You ate the course food I ate. You brought gladness to my heart! To others you may have given rich gifts. But to me you have given yourself!'

Points for Pro-Action

What is richer than giving the gift of oneself?

Love remains rhetoric when it lacks reality.

Empathy is putting oneself in the shoes of others.

Sympathy is common; empathy is uncommon. The world needs empathizers more than sympathizers - Shiv Khera.

61

Where the Mind Is Without Fear!

'Where the mind is without Fear' is one of the famous poems of Rabindranath Tagore. It was originally composed in Bengali, under the title 'Prarthana', meaning prayer. This poem appeared in the volume called 'Naibedya' in 1901. Tagore wrote this poem when India was under the clutches of British Rule. He wrote this poem to encourage the countrymen, to instill courage in their hearts and minds. The uniqueness of this work of Tagore was that it articulated more the significance of internal freedom which symbolizes unity, self-dignity, honesty, reasonableness and objectivity. At the time when the entire nation was craving for freedom from Britishers, Tagore's call to become internally free was not intelligible to many yet his realization that external freedom without internal freedom will be of no avail is true beyond any objection.

'Where the mind is without fear and the head is held high
Where knowledge is free
Where the world has not been broken up into fragments
By narrow domestic walls
Where words come out from the depth of truth
Where tireless striving stretches its arms towards perfection
Where the clear stream of reason has not lost its way
Into the dreary desert sand of dead habit
Where the mind is led forward by thee
Into ever-widening thought and action
Into that heaven of freedom, my Father, let my country awake.'

Points for Pro-Action

Without freedom from the past, there is no freedom at all, because the mind is never new, fresh, innocent – J. Krishnamurti.

A nation suffers when popular values become more important than values and justice – Shiv Khera.

The honest have a value; the corrupt have a price.

We get the kind of government we deserve.

62

Evil Can Never Beget Good!

One day, the Persian poet, Rumi Que Moavia, the first of the
Ommiad caliphs, was sleeping in his palace when he was woken
up by a strange man. 'Who are you?' he asked. 'I am Lucifer,'
came the reply. 'And what do you want?' 'It is the hour for prayers, and
yet you are still asleep.'

Moavia was amazed. Why was the prince of darkness, who seeks out the
souls of men of little faith, reminding him to fulfil his religious duties?

'Remember,' Lucifer explained, 'I was brought up as an angel of light.
Despite everything that has happened to me, I cannot forget my origins.
A man may travel to Rome or to Jerusalem, but he always carries the
values of his own country in his heart. Well, the same thing happens
with me. I still love the Creator, who nourished me when I was young
and taught me to do good. When I rebelled against him, it was not
because I did not love him; on the contrary, I loved him so much that
I felt jealous when he created Adam. At that moment, I wanted to defy
the Lord, and that was my downfall; nevertheless, I still remember the
blessings bestowed on me and hope that, perhaps, by doing good, I can
one day return to paradise.'

Moavia replied: 'I can't believe what you are saying. You have been
responsible for the destruction of many people on earth.' 'Well, you
should believe it,' insisted Lucifer. 'Only God can build and destroy,
because he is all-powerful. When he created man, he also created, as
part of life, desire, vengeance, compassion and fear. So, when you look

at the evil around you, don't blame me; I merely reflect back the bad things that happen.'

Moavia was sure that something was wrong, and he began to pray desperately to God to enlighten him. He spent the whole night talking and arguing with Lucifer; but despite the brilliant arguments he heard, he remained unconvinced.

When day was dawning, Lucifer finally gave in and said: 'You are right. When I came yesterday to wake you up so that you would not miss the hour of prayer, my intention was not to bring you closer to the Divine Light. I knew that if you failed to fulfil your obligations, you would feel profoundly sad and, over the next few days, would pray with twice the faith, asking forgiveness for having forgotten the correct ritual. In the eyes of God, each one of those prayers made with love and repentance would be equivalent to two hundred prayers said in an ordinary, automatic way. You would end up more purified and more inspired; God would love you more; and I would still be further from your soul.'

Lucifer vanished, and an angel of light took his place: 'Never forget today's lesson,' the angel said to Moavia. 'Sometimes evil comes disguised as an emissary of good, but its real intention is to cause more destruction.' On that day, and the days that followed, Moavia prayed with repentance, compassion and faith. His prayers were heard a thousand times by God.

Points for Pro-Action

Once I saw a captivating image with a caption: 'Your follower is not always your fan' (It was the image of a running deer chased by a lion!).

It takes just the crack of a soul for a person to be evil.

Evil has its cushion in the failures of a soul.

In the internal struggle between good and evil, the one who wins is often the one we feed.

63

Did I Tell You Not to Hiss?

In a certain village, a cobra bit and killed many people. The villagers complained to a holy man, whom they believed had miraculous powers over animals. The holy man called the cobra and ordered it not to bite anybody. Thereafter, the cobra entirely ceased its habit of biting people. But the time came when, because the cobra was quiet and harmless, the villagers started teasing it. Even the small boys pelted stones at it. The troubled cobra was now resentful of the holy man's command. It went over to him and complained about what was happening. The holy man was sympathetic. He commented: 'I asked you not to bite. Did I tell you not to hiss?'

Points for Pro-Action

The difference between pro-acting and reacting is choice.

Reaction is destructive; pro-action is constructive.

When we pro-act we are in control; when we react, we are controlled by.

Reaction is the act of a coward; uncultured mind; response is the act of a free man.

64

I Created You!

Apious man once started crying out to God in a tone of condemnation for the apparent thriving of evil and injustice. 'Oh, God! Why are you silent? Why do you turn your blind eye? Why can't you do something about it? God replied, 'My son I did intervene to stop the spread of evil and injustice?' taken aback, he asked God, 'Tell me what did you do?' God answered: 'I created you.'

Points for Pro-Action

Blaming others is excusing yourself – Robin Sharma.

Unless we stop the blame game, the desire is to blame the other and to make them responsible.

Taking responsibility for our actions is the first sign of empowering oneself.

The proactive approach to a mistake is to acknowledge it instantly, correct and learn from it – Stephen Covey.

65

Master's Heir!

Before leaving the world, a master wanted to appoint one of his trusted disciples as a successor to the school he was running. Therefore, he placed an open invitation for his disciples to appear for the contest if they ever felt worthy to succeed him. He had hundreds of disciples. Only five persons stood up. He laughed and said, 'You are the ones who have missed me, so just get out of the school and get lost.' Then he went through the crowd of disciples, looking into each disciple's eyes, and he found four persons. He brought them out and he said, 'I am going to ask a single question. The answer is going to decide who will be my representative, when I am gone. What is the essence of my whole mystic approach? Just use the minimum words. The first man said, 'It is meditation.' The master said, 'You have my skin. You have penetrated me only skin deep. Just get back to your seat.' And he asked the second man, 'What is your answer?' The second man said, 'Enlightenment.' The master said, 'You have my bones; just get back to your place.' The third person said, 'Master, I do not know.' The master said, 'You have my very marrow. It is good, but not good enough; you still know something. Just go and sit down.' He looked at the fourth man. The man had just tears in his eyes, no words. He fell at the feet of his master who then said, 'You have been chosen, you will represent me. You have my being. You have got it – what they cannot say with words, you have said by your silence. What they cannot say...although one of them came very close when he said, 'I do not know,' deep inside himself he was full of pride of not knowing, he was full of knowing that 'I don't know.' What he could not say, you managed to say loudly with your tears.'

Points for Pro-Action

There are some mysteries that cannot be verbalized; rather than trying to unfurl them, let us learn to cherish them.

The mystery of human life is not a problem to be solved but a reality to be experienced.

Mystery is like horizon. The nearer we go, the farther it moves.

There are some things for which we only need surrender.

But I Am Not Hollering About It!

An old man was seated relaxed on a riverbank. All ofa sudden, there was a loud cry from the one who was drowning in the river. 'Help, I can't swim! I can't swim!' he cried. 'I can't either,' said the old man sitting on the riverbank chewing tobacco. 'But I'm not hollering about it!'

Points for Pro-Action

It is always easy to be an outsider and pass judgement.

Good judgement requires insider's perspective which would mean to put ourselves in the shoes of others.

Sometimes we emphasize more upon being reasonable that we forget about being human.

Helping someone on request is good; but better still is perceiving the need and helping unasked.

67

Bricks of Attention!

'**A**re you crazy? You have ruined my new car. I will have to pay lots of money to repair it' shouting angrily the executive came out of his car. Then shaking the lad ferociously, he shouted at the top of his voice 'why did you throw that brick?' 'Sorry, sorry' said the boy in total shock. 'My handicapped brother has fallen out of his wheelchair and I can't lift him up; he is too heavy. I waved down but nobody cared to stop. I didn't know what else to do. So, I thought the best thing would be to throw a brick. Will you help me?' Tears flowed down the boy's cheeks. He pointed around the parked car his fallen brother and the empty wheelchair nearby. At this, the executive's anger suddenly evaporated into thin air. He set the wheelchair upright, then lifted the handicapped youngster into it. He took long, slow strides back to his Esteem, then drove off. He decided not to repair the dent. He kept it there to remind him that modern life is so hectic that one must throw bricks to call someone's attention.

Points for Pro-Action

We have grown too indifferent that some people must throw bricks at us to grab our attention.

The mechanized world has turned us into mechanized humans.

Money has taken the place of relationships, solidarity and concern for the other.

Unfortunately, we are yet to realize that at the end of our life, our worth will be valued more in terms of the relations that we would have built rather than the money we would have earned.

68

Fall and Get Up Again!

When someone asked an Orthodox monk what the monks were doing in the monastery, he replied, 'Fall and get up again, fall and get up again, fall and get up again.' The answer looks quite amusing, although it is not without a deep meaning attached to it.

Points for Pro-Action

Smooth sea never makes a skilful mariner.

A ship at the dock is safe; but that is not what the ship is built for.

Adversity is the best teacher.

Falling is not a weakness; but refusing to get up surely is.

69

Love Is Sufficient unto Love!

Khalil Gibran echoes characteristics of love by his song on love. 'When love beckons to you, follow him, though his ways are hard and steep. And when his wings enfold you yield to him, though the sword hidden among his pinions may wound you. And when he speaks to you believe in him, though his voice may shatter your dreams as the north wind lays waste the garden. For even as love crowns you so shall he crucify you. Even as he is for your growth so is he for your pruning. Even as he ascends to your height and caresses your tenderest branches that quiver in the sun, so shall he descend to your roots and shake them in their clinging to the earth. Like sheaves of corn he gathers you unto himself. He threshes you to make you naked. He sifts you to free you from your husks. He grinds you to whiteness. He kneads you until you are pliant. And then he assigns you to his sacred fire, that you may become sacred bread for God's sacred feast… Love gives naught but itself and takes naught but from itself. Love possesses not nor, would it be possessed. For love is sufficient unto love.'

Points for Pro-Action

Love is the catalyst for change in the individual as well as the society.

Love had achieved what hatred could never touch upon.

Love as a culture can cure the ills of our society.

It is not that we employ love in us as a feature; rather we are employed by love as its agents.

What Would He Do If He Ever Caught One?

A farmer had a dog who used to sit by the roadside waiting for vehicles to come around. As soon as one came, he would run down the road, barking and trying to overtake it. One day a neighbour asked the farmer 'Do you think your dog is ever going to catch a car?' The farmer replied, 'That is not what bothers me. What bothers me is what he would do if he ever caught one.'

Points for Pro-Action

Why I do what I do is more important in appraisals.

If we don't know where we are going, any road will take us there.

If we have not found something larger than ourselves, probably we have failed to figure out our purpose in life.

Our efforts should have a purpose as a brook joins to a river and a river to a sea.

Fear Kills!

A Zen story goes thus: A man walking in the night slipped and fell from a rocky path. Afraid he would fall down thousands of feet, because he knew that just at the edge of the path was a very deep valley, he grabbed hold of a branch that was overarching the edge. In the darkness of night all he could see below his feet was a bottomless abyss. He shouted, and his own shout was reflected – there was nobody to hear him. Throughout the night, the man, not having even one near him to share the mental agony and pain of fear suffered and endured the night of torture. Every moment there was death below, his hands were becoming cold, he was losing his grip, but he managed to hold on, and as the sun came out, he looked down and he laughed! There was no abyss. Just six inches below his feet there was a rock ledge. He could have rested the whole night, slept well – the ledge was big enough – but instead, the whole night was a nightmare.

Points for Pro-Action

The story teaches that often our fear is not more than six inches deep.

There is a book titled 'Kill Fear Before It Kills You' authored by J.P. Vaswani.

Fear of pain destabilises us than the pain itself.

Often it is true that we feed our fear.

72

Death in Teheran!

There is a story by name *Death in Teheran* and it runs like this. A rich mighty Persian walked in his garden with his servant who said he encountered death and was terrified and therefore pleaded his master to give him his fastest horse so that he could escape to Teheran. Getting the fastest horse, he wanted, the servant travelled in haste to Teheran. That same evening, on his departure, the master himself met death and asked why he terrified his servant. Death replied, 'I did not threaten him; I only showed surprise in still finding him here when I planned to meet him tonight in Teheran.'

Points for Pro-Action

There are two ways of responding to a situation: fight or flight. Instead of fighting the situation, many take recourse to flight only to find the situation worse later than what it was earlier.

Running away from the reality hardly helps us to solve the situation. What could have been easily solved gets multiplied by our act of escaping it.

We must learn to face what is inevitable rather than flee from them.

The fact of our temporariness should confer on us the perspectives of preparing for the everlasting life.

73

The Moment of Dawn!

A rabbi gathered together his students and asked them: 'How do we know the exact moment when night ends and day begins?' 'When it's light enough to tell a sheep from a dog', said one boy. Another student said: 'No, when it is light enough to tell an olive tree from a fig tree.' 'No, that's not a good definition either.' 'Well, what's the right answer?' asked the boys, and the Rabbi said: 'When a stranger approaches, and we think he is our brother, and all conflicts disappear, that is the moment when night ends and day begins.'

Points for Pro-Action

The moment of dawn is when we realize that all the rest of the humanity is our brethren.

It arrives with our awareness that all discriminations are human made and injustices are born of hatred towards the other.

We should join hands to fight the menace of division in the name of caste, creed and colour.

Let us concentrate upon what can unite us than what can divide us. That is nobility and greatness.

The One Upon My Back Is My Brother!

As he was walking on the street a man came upon a little boy who carried his disabled brother upon his back. The man grew concerned about the sight but still concluded it must have been a heavy burden for the little boy to bear with. Therefore, he commented 'That's a heavy burden for you to carry.' Contrary to his expectations, the boy replied 'That is not a burden at all. The one upon my back is my brother.'

Points for Pro-Action

What is done in love is not burdensome; it is a labour of love.

The sacrifice done with all goodwill endures the pain gladly.

Burden is often in relation to what we carry and how much we love it.

You cannot escape the responsibility of tomorrow by evading it today – Abraham Lincoln.

The Capacity to Suffer!

Once there was a general who was infamous for his brutality. He was vicious without mercy. He went to attack a small village that lay in the path of his army. Everyone in the village, knowing of the general's reputation, ran away – everyone except one man. When the general entered the village, he found this one man sitting calmly under a tree. So, the general went up to the man and said, 'Do you know who I am, and do you know what I am capable of? I can run my sword right through you without batting an eye!' And the man said, 'I know.' Looking at the general, he continued, 'But do you know who I am and what I am capable of? I will let you do it without batting an eye.'

Points for Pro-Action

Who is stronger - the one who inflicts pain or the one who endures it without any grumbling? Here lies the difference between the brave and the coward.

Usually sufferings are of two kinds – one due to our inability and the other due to our convictions. It is not out of our inability that we are called to suffer but for the sake of our convictions towards establishing justice.

By this we know, why we suffer, who causes the suffering and why we should continue to suffer without opposition.

To suffer for a cause is nobler than anything else.

76

Blind One of My Eyes!

In a village there lived two neighbours, always vying with each other for anything. Either the first one was jealous of the second one or vice versa. Never was there a time when they appreciated each other's growth and blessings from God. Once, both decided to fast and pray in order to win God's favour. Not willing to disappoint both and at the same time wanting to put an end to their attitude of jealousy, God appeared to them to grant the boons they prayed for but on one condition that if one of them asks for a favour, the other would be blessed with a double fold. Having this in mind, the first man asked for five acres of land only to find his neighbour in possession of ten acres. Again, when he asked for a beautiful house, the other had two of them. He lost his cool and said enough is enough. Now the first man burning with jealousy, asked God to blind one of his eyes.

Points for Pro-Action

Jealousy takes pleasure in the fall of others.

It calculates not in terms of how one has been blessed but how one has been cursed in comparison to the other.

Moreover, it is a refusal to count one's blessings.

It never wills the welfare of others; rather it abolishes the consideration of others.

The Wisdom of The Judge!

Apoor old woman was running a small tiffin shop in which she prepared and sold edibles and eatables. With nobody to care for her in her declining years, she had to earn her living thus. Once a thief stole her paltry income and left her in distress. She lodged a complaint on him and he was summoned to the court. On being enquired if he stole her money, he denied the charge with all his might, pleading to the judge that the coins in his possession were earned from the sweat of his brow. The wise judge would not budge an inch and he ordered for the rupee coins to be thrown into a bucket of water. As oil does not mingle with water, the entire bucket formed an oily layer making everybody understand that the coins were that of the old woman and the judge ordered the thief to be punished.

Points for Pro-Action

Theft is stealing someone's labour and feasting on someone's sweat.

The haves are morally responsible for the have-nots of the society.

Accumulation of wealth by improper means and profiteering is nothing less than theft itself.

There is enough for everyone's need and not for everyone's greed – MK Gandhi.

Puppy Will Need Someone Who Understands!

It was a shop in which puppies were available for sale. A crippled boy entered the shop and looked for his choice of a puppy. All of them were separated according to their prices. He noticed a dog with a lesser price tag although the same kind was sold for a higher price. When he enquired why it was so, the shopkeeper answered him that it costs less because it was crippled. The boy decided to buy that dog for the same price as that of others of its kind. Noticing the surprising glance of the shopkeeper he said, 'Well, I do not run so well myself, and the little puppy will need someone who understands.'

Points for Pro-Action

The little boy's act of sensitivity would certainly surpass all the rhetoric on kindness.

Kindness is always in proportion to our acts to justify it.

Goodness always requires a public posture.

Goodness grows in us like flowers grow in any garden; by being planted and watered and nourished.

79

Heart Full of Love!

In a village a young man had a beautiful heart, a heart without any dirt or a blemish. He grew proud of its beauty that one day he appeared in the public challenging people, 'Who has a heart that is more beautiful than mine?' To his surprise, when all the others hesitated, an elderly man came forward claiming that his heart would meet his challenge. The old man went on to make his heart visible but only to be frowned upon by his fellow bystanders gathered about because it was with much dirt, stitches and holes, contrary to that of the young man. However, the old man was not discouraged but rather began to explain himself. 'The dirt on my heart refers to the disrespect my love had accumulated over the years. Similarly, the stitches mean that the love I lavished upon others, was hardly returned in the same measure. Not finding the returns adequate, I had to stitch my heart to make it a whole. Sadly, the holes you find are signs of unrequited love. They were so willing to cherish my love but never cared to pay it back to me that with nothing to make them up, I have left them to remain as holes.' On listening to the old man's explanation, the youngster realized the truth and regretted the fact that his heart was never use.

Points for Pro-Action

Often, love meets with rejection; a heart full of love is also a heart full of pain.

A heart that has never suffered for the love of the other may not have understood the value of love at all.

The primary meaning of love lies in its capacity to sacrifice.

Every one of us is but the product of sacrifices.

80

I Am Starting to Forget!

S oon after her brother was born, Sachi asked her parents to be out in order that she could be alone with the baby. Thinking that the four-year-old would be jealous of him, they were behind the door watching. She said, 'Baby, tell me what God feels like. I am starting to forget.'

Points for Pro-Action

Every child comes with the message that God is not yet discouraged of humanity – Rabindranath Tagore.

Each of us is made up of both the material and the divine. Unfortunately, we are so busy with our materiality that we often forget our divinity.

Not because of their disbelief they are atheists! But because they have not found God in the life of theists.

Real faith in God culminates with allowing the Divine to surface in all that we do.

81

Give Me A Word!

'*D*uc verbum' ('Give me a word'), the seeker said, and the elder responded to the disciple with a wisdom saying meant to be explored in all its ramifications, 'Go into your cell and your cell will teach you everything.'

Points for Pro-Action

The problem today is that we are willing to be more external than internal.

Being in touch with our being is the most essential thing we need today.

The restless heart betrays itself with restless and reckless acts.

If we have the courage to go into ourselves, we can come face to face with all that disturbs us.

Is There Life Before Death?

Once upon a time, a group of disciples asked the elder, 'Holy One, give us the answer to the greatest spiritual question of them all: is there life after death?' And the elder smiled. 'Ah, my friends,' the elder said, 'the question you ask is an interesting one, but it is not the greatest spiritual question of them all. The greatest spiritual question of them all is not, 'Is there life after death?' The greatest spiritual question of them all is, 'Is there life before death?'

Points for Pro-Action

We are often spent in comprehending the mysteries of life than really trying to understand how to live the life in the now.

A bird in the hand is worth two in the bush.

Let's not be discouraged by death but be encouraged by life.

The perpetual work of your life is but to lay the foundation of death – Michel de Montaigne.

83

My Sermon Was Half Good!

O nce upon a time a rabbi returned to his home from the service in the synagogue, obviously tired, clearly disheartened. 'And how was your sermon?' his wife asked. 'Oh, my sermon was half good,' the rabbi said and sighed. 'And what was missing?' his wife asked. 'Well,' the rabbi said, 'I now have the poor willing to take. But I am not sure that I have the rich as willing to give.'

Points for Pro-Action

If contemplation is coming to see as God sees, then contemplation without confrontation with the self about the world and our place in it is not enough.

Life hereafter without life here is a humbug.

Encouragement of the poor without the commitment of the rich is absurd.

Our commitment towards the last and the least should be born of the willingness to empower them.

Change Is Important!

'Holy one,' the disciple said, 'how many people have you cured?' 'Oh, almost none,' the Holy One said. 'But that can't be true', the disciple protested. 'People come to you from everywhere.' 'Ah, that's true,' the Holy One said, 'but most people don't come to be cured. They come to feel better. If they really wanted to be cured, they would have to change.'

Points for Pro-Action

Change of heart and healing go together.

Most of the storms of life we could calm easily – if we ever really did something to change ourselves in the situation.

Change is not compromising; it is submitting oneself in the interest of becoming someone better.

There is a saying: Yesterday I was clever, so I wanted to change the world. Today I am wise, so I am changing myself.

We Will Be the Same As Them!

Apowerful wizard who wanted to destroy an entire kingdom, placed a magic potion in the well from which all the inhabitants drank. Whoever drank that water would go mad.

The following morning, the whole population drank from the well and they all went mad, apart from the king and his family, who had a well set aside for them alone, and which the magician had not managed to poison. The king was worried and tried to control the population by issuing a series of edicts governing security and public health. The policemen and the inspectors, however, had also drunk the poisoned water and they thought the king's decisions were absurd and resolved to take no notice of them.

When the inhabitants of the kingdom heard these decrees, they were convinced that the king had gone mad and was now giving nonsensical orders. They marched on the castle and called for his abdication.

In despair, the king prepared to step down from the throne, but the queen stopped him, saying: 'Let us go and drink from the communal well. Then, we will be the same as them.'

And that was what they did: the king and the queen drank the water of madness and immediately began talking nonsense. Their subjects repented at once; now that the king was displaying such wisdom, why not allow him to continue ruling the country?

The country continued to live in peace, although its inhabitants behaved very differently from those of its neighbours. And the king was able to govern until the end of his days.

Points for Pro-Action

Our willingness to be different should dare to face ridicule and embarrassment.

Winners don't do different things; they do things differently– Shiv Khera.

Being different is the hallmark of success.

Doing the same thing over and over expecting different results is called insanity.

86

Seagull and Mouse!

A seagull was flying over a beach, when it saw a mouse. It flew down and asked the mouse: 'Where are your wings?' each animal speaks its own language, and so the mouse didn't understand the question, but stared at the two strange, large things attached to the other creature's body. 'It must have some illness,' thought the mouse. The seagull noticed the mouse staring at its wings and thought: 'Poor thing. It must have been attacked by monsters that left it deaf and took away its wings.' Feeling sorry for the mouse, the seagull picked it up in its beak and took it for a ride in the skies. 'It is probably homesick' the seagull thought while they were flying. Then, very carefully, it deposited the mouse once more on the ground. For some months afterwards, the mouse was sunk in gloom; it had known the heights and seen a vast and beautiful world. However, in time, it grew accustomed to being just a mouse again and came to believe that the miracle that had occurred in its life was nothing but a dream.

Points for Pro-Action

To stay in one's loftiness requires greater strength and ability.

No one can pretend for too long because our inability will betray us one day.

Why to crawl when we can spread our wings?

Let's not stop our movement upwards.

87

There Would Be No One To Say,
"This Is A World!"

In his book, *The Pedagogy of the Oppressed*, Paulo Freiro shares this insightful conversation between an educator and an 'ignorant' farmer. 'In one of our culture circles in Chile, the group was discussing the anthropological concept of culture. In the midst of the discussion, a peasant who by 'banking standards' (In the banking concept of education, knowledge is a gift bestowed by those who consider themselves knowledgeable upon those whom they consider knowing nothing. A student learns only from a teacher and a teacher has nothing to learn from him/her) was completely ignorant said: 'Now I see that without man there is no world.' When the educator responded: 'Let's say, for the sake of argument, that all the men on earth were to die, but that the earth itself remained, together with trees, birds, animals, rivers, seas, the stars. ... wouldn't all this be a world?' 'Oh no,' the peasant replied emphatically. 'There would be no one to say: 'This is a world.''

Points for Pro-Action

The reply of the peasant startles the educator who operates with the mindset of 'I know everything' and 'you know nothing.'

With good teaching the esteem of the student goes up and not the feeling of his/her inadequacy.

Teaching is not imposing one's ideas; it is rather excavating the riches of the student.

Educating is empowering.

Delights To Cherish

God Has Blessed You!

Aminister was driving to the country when he came across a truly glorious farm being tended to by a lone farmer. Keen to remind the farmer of the source of his blessings, the Minister pulled over to the side of the road and called the farmer over. 'The Lord has blessed you with a beautiful farm,' said the minister. After a few moments' reflection, the farmer nodded his assent. 'He certainly has, reverend– but you should have seen it when he had it all to himself!'

Points for Pro-Action

God is not going to do for you and me what we can do for ourselves. God's blessing lets you begin; it is human effort that keeps it moving. The blessing of God is valued by human effort alone.

God helps those who help themselves.

God's blessing counts only in the context of our complementary efforts.

There is no substitute for hard work.

89

He Made the Wrong Choice!

A very learned philosopher dreamed that God appeared to him and offered him the choice between complete knowledge and complete happiness. Being a scholarly man, he chose complete knowledge. When asked to review what he had learned, he said he realised one thing; he had made the wrong choice.

Points for Pro-Action

Knowledge that is unable to act upon its learning is futile.

Sometimes we make choices. Sometimes choices make us.

Choice is what enables us to tell the world who we are.

We are our choices – Jean Paul Sartre.

The 52ⁿᵈ Problem!

A seeker journeyed through the furthest regions of the earth to find a teacher rumoured to know the secrets of happiness. When he arrived at the teacher's mountaintop retreat, he eagerly awaited his audience with the reclusive man. Finally, his moment came. 'Why have you come?' the teacher asked. The seeker proceeded to list problem after problem that he was facing in his life that the list went up to number 51. After listening patiently, the teacher sighed. 'I am afraid I can't help you with your problems.' 'Why not?' enquired the puzzled and disappointed seeker. 'Because the gods have decreed that we all must carry 51 problems with us at all times. Even if I could help you solve the problems you tell me of, they would only be replaced with 51 more.' The teacher paused to allow the full significance of the idea to sink in. 'I may, however,' he continued, 'be able to help you with your 52ⁿᵈ problem.' 'What is that?' asked the seeker. 'Your 52ⁿᵈ problem,' replied the teacher, 'is that you think you should not have the first 51 problems.'

Points for Pro-Action

These mountains that you are carrying, you were only supposed to climb – Najwa Zebian.

Our problem in life is that we always look for short-cuts and easy way-outs.

One bad chapter doesn't mean your story is over.

Let us not pray to God for a life without problems; rather the strength to face them.

The Fox and The Sour Grapes!

A successful CEO expressed this irony in the form of a sequel to the fable of the fox and the grapes. The fox, failing to reach the grapes, 'rejected' it as sour. His friends, however, said he had failed and so he was calling the grapes sour. The humiliated fox was provoked into action – while his friends slept, he worked hard for long hours, practising the high jump. One day, as his friends watched, he jumped and deftly grabbed the grapes. The fox earned their respect and titles were conferred upon him. The poor fox, however, discovered to his dismay that the grapes he'd managed to attain were in fact sour. How could he reject it now? Would he not be jeered at? The fox had reached the point of no return; he must feed on, pretending to eat the sour grapes with great relish. Miserable and unable to share his secret, the fox eventually fell ill and died.

Points for Pro-Action

Being yourself is not a sign of weakness; it is imitation. Being yourself is a strength. We have not come into the world to be mere copies of others.

One should always rejoice about the joy of being oneself.

There is a sharp difference between drawing inspiration and blind imitation; the former is desirable; the latter despicable.

Living to meet the expectations of others ultimately destroys who we really are.

A Glass of Water And A Loaf Of Bread!

Agreat sage asked a prosperous king, 'If you were about to die of thirst and starvation and someone offered you a glass of water and a loaf of bread in exchange for your wealth and kingdom, would you give them to him?' 'Of course, I would,' replied the king. 'Anybody would.' 'Then why,' asked the sage, 'have you wasted your entire life amassing all this land and wealth when they are worth no more to you than a glass of water and a loaf of bread?'

Points for Pro-Action

Human ambitions are meaningless when they cannot lead us to realize that happiness is more internal.

To be ambitious is not wrong in itself; but when it robs us of your happiness and peace, it is.

Do we ever have the time to realize, 'What are we running after?'

Life should not be reduced to material hunt; it is a meaning-making process.

The Elephant and The Crow!

A crow and elephant were friends and the elephant became little envious of the crow's ability to fly and expressed his wish to fly like crow. And the crow gave confidence to the elephant. The crow reached back with his beak and pulled a feather off his tail. Giving it to the elephant the crow said, 'All you have to do is hold the feather firmly with your trunk and flap your huge ears as hard as you can. That will do the trick. If you don't believe me try it.' The elephant then tried it and flew freely high above the trees. He sailed over towns and villages and surveyed the people below. He became so happy and finishing his journey the elephant gave the feather back to the crow. 'Oh, the feather! Said the crow. 'Well, as a matter of fact, it wasn't really necessary, you know. It was one I was going to discard anyways. To tell you the truth, there is no power in the feather. It was the flapping of your ears that made you fly. But I knew if I had told you that, you would have thought it ridiculous and would not have tried at all. So, I had to give you something to believe in and what better thing than this feather!'

Points for Pro-Action

Great achievement is to give hope to others.

Good motivators are those in whose presence we feel confident about ourselves.

It requires someone's help to teach us to believe in ourselves; to believe in who we are and what we can do.

It would be rather fruitful if we can help others find meaning in their lives.

94

Leave This Chanting and Singing!

This poem of Tagore challenges our piety. He advises the priests to give up their counting of beads and their singing and chanting of mantras. He also urges them to stop the worship of God in a secluded corner of the temple, with their eyes half shut. God is not to be found in this way. God lives with the humble and down-trodden. He lives with those who toil in sun and shower and whose clothes are soiled with dust. By this, Tagore glorifies the life of humble labourers and rejects meaningless piety. He conveys that participation in the activity of life is essential for the realization of God. This poem earned its acclaim due to its condemnation of the pseudo-zeal of worshippers everywhere.

'Leave this chanting and singing and
Telling of beads! Whom dost thou worship
in this lonely dark corner of a
Temple with doors all shut? Open
Thine eyes and see thy God is not before thee!
He is there where the tiller is tilling
The hard ground and where the path-maker
Is breaking stones. He is with them
In sun and in shower, and his garment is covered with dust. Put off
Thy holy mantle and even like him come
Down on the dusty soil!
Deliverance? Where is this deliverance
To be found? Our master himself
Has joyfully taken upon him the bonds of

Creation; he is bound with us all forever.
Come out of thy meditations and
Leave aside thy flowers and incense!
What harm is there if thy clothes
Become tattered and stained? Meet
Him and stand by him in toil and in
Sweat of thy brow.'

Points for Pro-Action

Piety does not lead us to forgetfulness of this world and the misery that surrounds human lives; it rather empowers us with mindfulness to be sensitive to the needs of the other.

Piety makes us find God in the other with whom we are living. It makes us perceive that the God whom we are trying to worship is present flesh and blood in our neighbours.

The more pious we grow, the better persons we should become.

Our piety should help us realize that our neighbours are the invisible face of God.

The Heir's Portrait!

A very wealthy man was heart-broken when his wife died leaving behind their young son. Fortunately, he could depend on a very affable housekeeper who took care of the child as her own. When the lad was barely twenty, however, he met with a tragic death. His father was so grief-stricken that his health began to dwindle, and he, too, died a few months later, in the loving arms of the housekeeper. He had, no doubt, made adequate provision for her.

The millionaire left no will, and since no living heir to his enormous estate could be traced, the whole property was taken over by the state. Eventually an auction was arranged to dispose of the personal effects of the mansion. The old housekeeper was present at the auction, not so much to bid for anything as to have a last glance at the things she had been familiar with for years. Among the several objects on display, there was one that attracted her attention; it was the photograph of the boy in his late teens. It was practically the only item that had no takers, so the woman paid the amount the auctioneer demanded and bought it for keepsakes.

While she dusted the frame at home, some papers fell out the back. They looked important, so she showed them to a lawyer-friend. The lawyer could not believe what he saw. He looked at the woman and said cheerfully: 'You've hit the jackpot, dear. Your old master has left all his property and savings to the person who loved his son enough to buy the picture.'

Points for Pro-Action

To live in hearts we leave behind is not to die – Thomas Campbell.

The hardest part of love is not losing someone; it is learning to live without the person.

It is true that the broken will always be able to love harder than most.

Real love reaches out even when there is no reason to love.

It Makes A Difference to This One!

There was a man taking a morning walk at the beach. He saw that along with the morning tide came hundreds of starfish and when the tide receded, they were left behind and with the morning sunrays, they would die. The tide was fresh, and the starfish were alive. The man took a few steps, picked one and threw it into the water. He did that repeatedly. Right behind him there was another person who could not understand what this man was doing. He caught up with him and asked, 'What are you doing? There are hundreds of starfish. How many can you help? What difference does it make?' This man did not reply; took two more steps, picked up another one, threw it into the water, and said, 'it makes a difference to this one.'

Points for Pro-Action

The meaning of life is to find your gift; the purpose of life is to give it away – Pablo Picasso.

Life is an opportunity to prove how we can impact human lives by the value of our own.

The sole meaning of life is to serve humanity – Leo Tolstoy.

Living is about bringing meaning to someone's life.

Thanks Dad!

One day a very wealthy father took his son on a trip to the country for the sole purpose of showing his son how it was to be poor. They spent a few days and nights on the farm of what would be considered a very poor family. After their return from the trip, the father asked his son how he liked the trip. 'It was great, Dad,' the son replied. 'Did you see how poor people can be?' the father asked. 'Oh Yeah,' said the son.' 'So, what did you learn from the trip?' asked the father. The son answered: I saw that we have one dog and they had four; we have a pool that reaches to the middle of the garden and they have a creek that has no end; we have imported lanterns in our garden and they have the stars at night; our patio reaches to the front yard and they have the whole horizon; we have a small piece of land to live on and they have fields that go beyond our sight; we buy our food, but they grow theirs; we have walls around our property to protect us, they have friends to protect them.' The boy's father was speechless. Then his son added: 'Thanks Dad for showing me how poor we are.'

Points for Pro-Action

Beauty lies in the eyes of the beholder.

Sometimes reality is sadly a question of perception. Just because we are right does not mean others are wrong.

We don't see things as they are; we see them as we are.

'You just haven't seen life from my side' – Two people arguing over a number which to one is six and to the other nine. Who is right?

98

Philosophy of An Ant!

Attitude makes all the difference. It can make or break lives. We might understand it better by looking at the philosophy of an ant, who sets an example of how to look at an obstacle: Have you ever seen an ant sitting idle? Probably not. Why? Because:

1. Ants never sit idle. It is not in their nature. They are hard working.

2. Ants never quit. If we try to block their way, they will go up, down, sideways, but they will not stop. How long do they keep trying to overcome the obstacle? Till they find a way to rise above it. So, obstacles don't stop them. They persist.

3. Ants are far-sighted. They don't think only about summer in summer. They are busy collecting food and preparing for the winter. That's why they are in a rush all through the summer season. You never see an idle ant unless it is dead.

4. Ants have a work-life balance – they work during summer and rest during winter. They hibernate to conserve energy. They know when to stop working.

5. Ants are purpose-driven – their sole job is to look for food for their mates. They don't get distracted. They are focused.

6. Ants can carry big responsibilities – although ants are small, their contributions are big. They can handle up to hundred times their body weight.

The philosophy of an ant can be concluded in one sentence – they are hardworking, purpose-driven, and far-sighted; they don't quit, and they maintain great work-life balance. Attitude is a habitual way of thinking and feeling. It is a viewpoint, a frame of mind, a thinking process and a way of looking at things. It is our standpoint, our approach to things or our reaction to situations in life.

Points for Pro-Action

Sincere people relax more in industry than inactivity.

Sloth like rust consumes faster than labour wears - Benjamin Franklin.

Often additional responsibility is the reward for hard work and works well done.

The result of laziness would likely be that mediocrity takes the place of excellence, procrastination replaces priority and compromise becomes the way of life.

Grace Before Meals!

Ahunter was cornered by a lion and he had no bullets left in his gun. He had no alternative but to kneel and pray. If he was praying, nothing seemed to be happening. He then opened his eyes to see what happened to the lion. To his surprise, he found the lion praying. He asked the lion as to what it was doing? The lion said, 'I am saying grace before my meal.'

Points for Pro-Action

Prayer is not tuning God according to our imaginations and specifications.

Our imagination of God is often that God is a blessing-vending machine.

Prayer is to get to know the mind of God.

It is to be resolved to be godly. It is a resolution to fight against all that is ungodly.

Jaguar and Cat!

A jaguar persuaded a cat to teach him how to pounce. After a few successful experiments with bugs and insects, the jaguar, his appetite whetted, decided to try out this new technique on the cat itself. The cat, however, jumped out of danger like a flash, and the jaguar landed in a heap. 'That is not fair!' whined the jaguar. 'You did not teach me that trick.' 'A smart teacher,' the cat reminded him, 'never teaches a pupil all his tricks.'

Points for Pro-Action

The literal meaning of life is whatever you're doing that prevents you from killing yourself – Albert Camus.

Taking care of oneself does not mean 'me' first; it means 'me too.'

Self-care is a modern virtue. It is a priority.

After all, we need a wall to draw something on.